THE BOY AVIATORS IN AFRICA

OR

AN AERIAL IVORY TRAIL

Captain Wilbur Lawton

1st WORLD LIBRARY
Literary Society

The Boy Aviators in Africa

Captain Wilbur Lawton

© 1st World Library – Literary Society, 2005
PO Box 2211
Fairfield, IA 52556
www.1stworldlibrary.org
First Edition

LCCN: 2004195664

Softcover ISBN: 1-59540-816-9
Hardcover ISBN: 1-59540-815-0
eBook ISBN: 1-59540-817-7

Purchase *"The Boy Aviators in Africa"*
as a traditional bound book at:
www.1stWorldLibrary.org/purchase.asp?ISBN=1-59540-816-9

1st World Library Literary Society is a nonprofit
organization dedicated to promoting literacy by:

- Creating a free internet library accessible from any
  computer worldwide.
- Hosting writing competitions and offering book
  publishing scholarships.

Readers interested in supporting literacy
through sponsorship, donations or
membership please contact:
literacy@1stworldlibrary.org
Check us out at: www.1stworldlibrary.ORG
and start downloading free ebooks today.

The Boy Aviators in Africa

contributed by Tim, Ed & Rodney

in support of

1st World Library Literary Society

CHAPTER I

A REUNION

"Here, Harry, catch hold."

"Ouch - I dropped that cartridge box on my pet corn."

"Say, you fellows, are we going to Africa or are we on a Coney Island picnic?"

"Be serious now, Billy Barnes, you may be all right as a reporter, but as a shipping clerk you're no more good than a cold storage egg."

"Well, I'm doing the best I can," was the indignant reply, "here - I've got it all down: Box 10 - One waterproof tent, one rubber-blanket, tent-pegs, ropes, more ropes. - Say, Frank, what in the name of the 'London Times' and jumping horn-toads do you want so much rope for?"

"To tie up a certain young reporter named William Barnes when he gets too fresh," was the laughing reply.

The three boys sat about a heaped, confused collection of ammunition, cooking-utensils, rifles, and camp "duffle" in general, one evening late in May. The eldest of the group, a sunny-faced, clear eyed lad of about sixteen, held in his hand a notebook from which he called out the inventory of the articles piled about him as his brother, a youth of fourteen, sorted them out. The third member of the trio was a short, stocky chap of possibly seventeen, with sharp, blue eyes that gleamed behind a pair of huge spectacles. He was examining a camera with care; from time to time turning his attention to an open notebook that lay beside him in which he was supposed to be entering the list as the other called it off.

The place where the boys were busying themselves was the upper floor of a large garage in the rear of the Chester residence, on Madison Avenue, New York City, which had been turned into a workshop for the two young Chesters - Frank and Harry - already well known to our readers as The Boy Aviators. The well set-up lad who was so industriously calling off the equipment that lay scattered about was Frank Chester, and the ready classifier of the mixed-up outfit was Harry, his younger brother. The third member of the group was Billy Barnes, the young reporter, already down to us as the chronicler of the Chester boys' adventures in Nicaragua and the depths of the Everglades of Florida. Since the boys' return from Florida on the U. S. torpedo boat, the Tarantula, they had been busy putting into shape the rough working plans of the African hunting expedition they had planned as a sort of vacation.

The ample bonus the government had awarded them for their singularly clever work in rescuing Lieutenant Chapin, the inventor of Chapinite, by their aeroplane Golden Eagle II, had supplied them with ample funds for their trip. As for Billy Barnes (or "Our Special

Staff Correspondent, William Barnes," as he was now known), besides the sum realized from the sale of the rubies the boys found in the Quesal Cave in Nicaragua, the money the youthful scribe had made on writing up the boys' Florida adventures had provided him with a good fat nest-egg.

The natural stimulus given to the red-blooded Chester boys by Mr. Roosevelt's hunting adventures had a good deal to do, with their resolution to go to Africa. And now - after several weeks of work on getting together as good an outfit as was procurable - they were putting what Billy called "the finishing touches" on their accoutrements. Stacked in corners of the room were big chests painted blue and marked with the boys' names and neatly numbered in white painted characters. These cases contained the different sections of the Golden Eagle II, the aeroplane equipped with wireless, that had made history in Florida.

There were twenty of these cases besides the ones labeled "Camp Outfit," "Medical," "Armory Chest," "Grub Chest," and several nondescript ones containing the odds and ends that an expedition of the kind they planned would find indispensable. In some smaller boxes also were packed yards and yards of bright-colored cloth and calico, spangles, cheap jewelry and brass ornaments for use among the natives. In making up their outfit the boys had taken the advice of a well-known African traveler who had retired from his adventurous life to purchase a place in New Jersey, where he intended to spend his remain days. Through a mutual friend the boys obtained an introduction to him and his advice in selecting the outfit had been simply invaluable.

"Go easy, carry lots of quinine, don't waste ammunition, and count ten before you pick a quarrel with a native," had been his simply laid-down rules for getting along in Africa, and these rules the boys had determined to adhere to strictly.

"Say, is this going to be a hunting trip or an invasion of Africa?" inquired Billy, quizzically as Harry sorted out and Frank read off ceaselessly the apparently interminable inventory of the supplies of the Chester party. "I'm getting writer's cramp."

"A hunting party of course," laughed Frank, "but you know that hunters who go into the bush depending on their rifles usually come out a good deal thinner than when they went in.

"That's so," assented Billy, "but when we have a sixty-mile aeroplane like the Golden Eagle II we can easily fly out to civilization in case of necessity."

"Yes, if we have enough gasoline," assented Harry, "but how much can we carry into the bush?"

"Just enough for our purposes and no more," replied Frank, readily, "fortunately the soluble tablets of picric and glycerine will help out our supply materially. A few of these tablets dissolved in gasoline render the efficiency of one ordinary gallon equal to three; but I don't care to use them except in a case of absolute necessity as they are very hard on an engine."

"Then we can count on every gallon we carry being of triple efficiency?" asked Billy.

"Certainly," replied Frank, who had invented the

tablets in question, and which were an extremely useful addition to the equipment of the modern aviator. As the boys worked on and the equipment, as it was classified, was packed away in the cases assigned to each class of articles, there came a sharp knock at the door of the garage building and a servant entered with a special delivery letter to Frank. The boy tore it open eagerly and then gave a low whistle of astonishment.

"Read it out, Harry," he said, handing the missive to his brother. "It concerns all of us."

Harry took it and read as follows:

DEAR FRANK AND HARRY:

Shall be in town to-morrow morning with my father and Mr. Luther Barr, the well-known ivory importer. He has a communication of importance for you. What it is I am afraid to trust to writing, but you will know full details when you see us. Will you call at the Waldorf at ten-thirty and have breakfast? We can discuss the matter over the meal. All I can say now is that if the Golden Eagle is still in shape for her old-time stunts there is work ahead of her that will prove harder than anything she has yet tackled. However, I know you are not the chaps to balk at a little danger – particularly when exciting adventures are in the wind.

So long, then, till to-morrow:

"LATHROP EASLEY"

"Well, what do you know about that?" gasped Billy

Barnes, here we are fixing up for a nice little holiday trip to rest our shattered nerves, and here comes, a job along that looks as if we should have to work all summer."

"It certainly is curious," replied Frank musingly.

"What can Lathrop mean? Who is Luther Barr? I have heard the name but I cannot place him."

"Lathrop says he is an ivory importer," suggested Harry.

"Easy to find out," said the resourceful Billy. "Where's the 'phone book?"

Frank handed the volume to him from its hook beside the instrument.

"Ah - here we are," exclaimed Billy, as he ran his finger triumphantly down the "B" list. "Barr, Luther - that's our man, eh? Ivory importer, offices No. 42 Wall Street - home, White Plains."

"White Plains, that's where Lathrop's folks live," exclaimed Harry. "That's where he first became associated with the Golden Eagle."

"And turned out to be a good partner," added Frank.

"A jim dandy," agreed Billy. "I tell you boys, I've got a good nose for news and if there isn't some sort of a story back of Mr. Luther Barr and Lathrop's letter I'll eat my hat without sauce."

Any acceptance of the young reporter's generous offer

was interrupted by a sudden noise in the usually quiet street.

"I tell you the fare's a dollar!" the boys heard an angry voice declaim.

"'Tain't nothing of the kind or I'm a lubber - fifty cents is all I'll pay. I'll be horn-swoggled if you get a cent more, yer deep-sea pirate," was the indignant phrased reply.

Something in the voice was strangely familiar but the "horn-swoggled" settled it.

"Ben Stubbs," gasped all the, boys simultaneously and rushed out of the garage to the street.

Here they found a stoutly-built, crisp-bearded man with a face tanned to what Billy called a "weathered oak finish," arguing loudly with a taxicab chauffeur. The man was obdurate over his fare and just at, the boys came on the scene was suggesting that his equally determined passenger get back in the cab and take a ride to the police station.

"The sergeant will settle our dispute," he said angrily.

"What's the trouble, Ben?" exclaimed Frank, giving the angry man on the pavement a hearty slap on the back.

"Why, this here piratical craft," the other was beginning when suddenly he dropped the battered bag he carried and burst into a mighty roar - a regular Cape Horn hail.

"Back my topsails if it ain't you, Frank," he cried,

wringing the other's hands till the boy's arms were almost dislocated. "And you too, Harry, and keel haul me ef here ain't Billy too. Well, if it ain't good to see, you Chester boys again."

"Say, are you the Chester Boys - the Boy Aviators?" suddenly cut in the chauffeur in a respectful tone.

"We are," replied Frank, "why?"

"Oh, well," said the chauffeur, "then I'll let your friend off with fifty cents. I thought he was a 'greeny'."

With that, he calmly twisted the dial of the cab which registered $1.00 back to the fifty cent mark and coolly pocketed the coin the indignant Ben handed.

"Does that thing work backwards?" demanded the amazed old adventurer, as the taxi whizzed off before he could frame words to express his indignation.

"Not often," replied Billy with a laugh. "I guess that chap reads the papers and thought it wouldn't do him any good to try to fool a particular friend of the Boy Aviators."

"Well, boys, what are your plans?" demanded Ben, as - after the rugged fellow had been introduced to Mrs. Chester, a sweet-faced old lady, and Mr. Chester, a fine-looking, gray-haired man of about fifty - he and the boys sat in the garage discussing the African outfit.

"We hardly know now," replied Frank, and then in a few words he described Lathrop's letter and its contents.

"Wherever that boy is there's bound to be doings," remarked Ben, sententiously, when the young leader had finished. "Down in Florida when he wasn't tumbling into alligators' mouths or getting bit by serpents he was allers up to some mischief - you mark my words there's something in the wind now."

The boys talked late and long that night over the letter and what possible plan Mr. Barr, the ivory importer, could have to discuss that would be of interest to them, but they were able to arrive at no definite conclusion except that there was nothing to be done about it till morning.

As for Ben with his usual philosophic attitude toward mysteries, he filled his pipe and silently smoked. To those of our readers who have not met Ben this phase of his character may seem inexplicable, but to the boys Ben's passive acceptance of any situation had become quite familiar. Ever since they had rescued the rugged old adventurer from a marooned treasure-mine in Nicaragua and he had shared their strange adventures in Florida on the Chapin Rescue Expedition, the old man had become as much a part of their necessary equipment as the Golden Eagle itself. He had arrived that night in response to a telegraphed request to his cottage at Amityville on Long Island, where he cultivated an extensive farm - also part of the Quesal ruby profits - and devoted himself to fishing and hunting.

'The Boys' mere word, however, that they were off to Africa had been sufficient to arouse the old man's roving instinct and here he was on deck once more as active as a boy and almost as impatient for the start for the Dark Continent. Ben slept at the Chester's home that night and if his dreams were not as populated with visions of elephants, leopards, deer, huge snakes and pigmy savages as theirs it was not any lack of interest in the coming expedition that was responsible for it.

Captain Wilbur Lawton

CHAPTER II

THE STOLEN IVORY

"Will you please send this card up to Mr. Beasley's rooms and tell him that the visitors he was expecting are here?"

It was Frank Chester who spoke early the next day, as the boys, in response to Lathrop's letter, stood at the Waldorf desk. The clerk looked at them a little disdainfully. Frank and Harry Chester were not the sort of boys who devoted much time to thinking about clothes and while they both wore dark neat-fitting suits they certainly did look a little out of place among the pasty-faced, cigarette-smoking youths in loud-looking garments who constituted most of the young men with whom the clerk was in the habit of coming in contact.

"I don't think that Mr. Beasley can see you now, call later," he began, superciliously turning round to the letter-rack and sorting out the mail and putting each guest's letters in the proper box.

For a second an angry flush rose to Frank's face. The man's manner was enough to irritate any high spirited boy. But Frank Chester was not given to what Bill Barnes called "flying off the handle." He calmly took another card from his pocket and in a rather sharp voice, though his tones were even enough said:

"Are you going to send that card up at once or shall I call the room on the telephone?"

The clerk faced quickly about. The two youths he had looked upon as rather awkward country bumpkins, judging as he did from their tanned faces and broad shoulders, were evidently not to be trifled with. He glanced at the card as he rolled it up and handed it to a boy to be placed in a pneumatic tube and shot up to the fourth floor, on which Mr. Beasley and his party had taken rooms.

"Oh, you are the Chester boys?" he exclaimed with a strong accent on the "the" and in markedly more respectful tones.

"We are," said Frank with a smile which was reflected on his brother's face.

"I beg your pardon for keeping you waiting, I'm sure," said the clerk with an apologetic leer, meant to be an engaging smile.

"That's all right," said Frank shortly, turning away from the desk.

"Well, having your name in the paper does do you some good after all," remarked Harry with a laugh. "That fellow certainly turned a flip-flop, when he found out who we were."

Five minutes later the boys were ushered into the Beasley rooms and were busily engaged shaking hands and exchanging all sorts of boyish exclamations of welcome with Lathrop Beasley, a tall, rather slender youth who had been their companion in Florida. Like the boys, Lathrop was an accomplished aviator and wireless operator, although he had not the initiative or the sturdy pluck to perform the feats that they had. He was, however, a boy of considerable brain and skill and among the boy-aviators of the country held an enviable position.

"About your letter," began Frank when the first greetings were over.

"In a minute," replied Lathrop, "here's father now."

As he spoke, the portieres parted and a stout, fresh complexioned gentleman, ruddy from his bath and shaving, appeared. He had the pompous manner of the successful man of business and seemed to the Chester boys to be the least bit patronizing in his manner.

"Mr. Barr will be here in a minute," he said, after introductions had been made by Lathrop, "he will explain to you his idea. I am merely a partner in the enterprise. You will, of course, be glad to accept any restrictions he may impose?"

"We hardly care to discuss that yet," said Frank, rather nettled by Mr. Beasley's pompous manner, "until we know what he requires." He exchanged glances with Harry.

"In fact," he went on, "we were planning to take a complete rest and follow in Mr. Roosevelt's foot-steps, by taking a hunting trip in Africa, only," he added with a smile, "we meant to hunt by aeroplane."

"Wonderful," said Mr. Beasley, evidently much impressed by Frank's ready manner, "when I was a boy, if a lad had a "bone-shaker" bicycle he thought he was doing something fine, and as for flying - why, we never thought of it."

"Perhaps the boys of to-day are further sighted," said Frank with quiet note of sarcasm in his tone that was quite lost on the well-meaning old merchant. Indeed at that moment Mr. Beasley rose heavily from his chair and stepped forward to greet a new arrival who appeared from another room of the suite.

"This is Mr. Luther Barr, the famous ivory importer," he said, with far more respect in his tones than he had used to the boys; whom indeed, he looked upon as talented chaps, but still boys - which to men of his caliber is an infallible sign that anything such youthful persons may attempt is extremely likely to go wrong. How erroneous such an opinion is, those of our readers who have followed the adventures of the Chester boys know.

Mr. Luther Barr deserves a new paragraph. Long, lean and hollow cheeked, the term "gangling" fits him better than any other. Mr. Luther Barr's black suit hung on him as baggily as the garments of a cornfield scarecrow and Mr. Luther Barr's sharp features were not improved by a small growth of gray hair; of the kind known as a "goatee" that sprouted from his lower rip. For the rest of the boys noticed that Mr. Barr was gifted with a singularly gimlet-like pair of steely blue eyes that seemed to bore through you.

"As sharp a man as ever drove up the price of ivory," added Mr. Beasley as he introduced the boys to this singular figure, "he can scent an ivory bargain - "

"From here to Africa," struck in Mr. Barr in a sharp nasal tone that grated unpleasantly, "and you and I are going to be Kings of Wall Street if these boys put this deal through for us," he added with what was meant to be an amiable smile, but which, as a matter of fact, distorted his face till it looked uncommonly like an old Japanese war mask. Indeed the boys, who had seen the collection in the Metropolitan Museum, could not help smiling to themselves, as the same thought struck each of them.

"Well, Beasley," exclaimed Barr suddenly, "I'm as sharp set as a Long Island fox. Let's have a bite of breakfast and then we can get down to business."

From Mr. Barr's manner of dispatching his breakfast and the remarkable skill with which he wielded his knife, in conveying various morsels to his mouth, it was evident that he had spent so much time piling up money that his social education had been sadly neglected. Once or twice the boys caught Lathrop's eye and they saw that the lad was blushing with shame at the uncouth manners of his father's friend. For this reason the boys refrained from paying any apparent attention to Mr. Barr's actions, although - as, they remarked afterwards - he was as well worth watching as the "sword swallower in a circus side show."

"Yes, boys," said Mr. Barr with his mouth full of buttered toast and ham and eggs, "I guess I know more about Africa than any man alive."

"You have crossed that continent?" asked Frank..

"No, sir," replied the old ivory merchant with some contempt. "I wouldn't waste my time where there ain't no ain't no money. What I mean is, I know more about the Gold Coast, the Ivory Coast and the Slave Coast than any man in this or any other country and have got more good solid coin out of them."

Mr. Beasley looked up admiringly from his plate. Here was evidently a man after his own heart.

"The Slave Coast?" echoed Harry inquiringly, "I thought - "

"Thought there wasn't no more slaves, eh?" inquired Mr. Barr amiably, swallowing his coffee with a noise like water running out of a bath tub, "wall, that's because yer young. When yer git older you'll larn that there's money in everything here's a demand for, and there's just as big a demand for slaves on some rubber plantations I could tell yer of as there ever was in the old days of the South - and more money in 'em on account of its being more dangerouser."

"Do you mean to say that there is slave-running now?" asked Mr. Beasley, while both Frank and Harry wondered and Lathrop looked uncomfortable.

"Sure I do," chirped Mr. Barr, "but no more for me. There's too many British gunboats and 'Merican gunboats and Dutch gunboats and what not about now to make it comfortable or healthy. No, I've retired from that business - but there's money in it," he concluded with a regretful sigh.

Immediately Mr. Barr had concluded his breakfast - and with his apparently slim accommodations it was a wonder to the boys where he put it all - he snapped, with a flinty glint of his small pig-like eyes:

"Now, let's git down to business. You boys want ter make a bit of money?"

"'To be sure we do," replied Frank, "but we don't want to make any that isn't honest money."

"We'll, there's no accounting for boys nowadays," sighed Mr. Barr, "however, you needn't worry about this money - there'll be plenty of it and it'll all be good honest coin."

"What do you wish us to do?" demanded Frank.

"Just this: Mr. Beasley here and me is in on a deal in ivory. That is, we were, but the big cache we had hoarded up in the Kuroworo Mountains in the Bambara country has been stolen by a rival trader, an Arab named Muley-Hassan. We know where he's hidden it and we know, too, that he won't dare to bring it out till he thinks that we aren't watching him. Now the time is ripe for a big deal in Ivory. There is a shortage in the market. Prices will go up sky high. If we get it out in time we'll make a barrel of coin, but if we don't we stand to lose heavily."

Mr. Beasley gave a groan; to the boys' amazement he seemed to be about to collapse. Lathrop too looked ill and anxious. Old Barr paid no attention, however, but went on.

"Now, I heard about you boys and your air-ship, and I heard, too, that you was planning a little trip to Africa and thought you might like to combine business and pleasure."

He drew from his pocket a much-thumbed, crudely drawn map and spread it out on the table. How he obtained it, the boys never learned exactly, but they heard later that a treacherous attendant of the ivory dealer had sold it to him for a good round sum.

"This country down here," he said, indicating it with a black rimmed finger nail, "is the Southern Soudan. Here's the Bambara country to the north of Uasule. Now right at this point, in the Moon Mountain range," - he pointed to a red-marked trail zigzagging across the map to the range and terminating in a red star - "right at that thar point, old Muley-Hassan, the Arab, has hidden our ivory cache. You see the latitude and longitude is marked and furthermore - and here's the most remarkable part of it - you will know the spot when you see it by the fact that the mountains above the cache present an exact facsimile of an upturned human face. In a direct line drawn from the nose of this face, where you see the red star, lies the ivory."

The boys were deeply interested. Unpleasant as was the impression old Barr had made on them, yet what he was disclosing was impressive; but as yet they did not show that they were anything more than casually struck by it.

"Well, Mr. Barr?" said Frank, as the old matt paused impressively.

"Well - " said Mr. Barr, "the scoundrel stole it and it's up to you to get it out of there, if you will undertake it."

"How does it depend on us?" asked Frank.

"In just this way. Muley-Hassan has his eye on us - - we can do nothing toward locating the ivory. You can pitch a camp there and scout about for it in your aeroplane or dirigible or whatever you call it."

"But even if we do find the Arab's hiding-place, what good does that do?" objected Frank.

"We can arrange with the French government to send soldiers up into the country and get the stuff out, if necessary," readily replied the wrinkled old ivory dealer, "but we can make no move till the cave is located. If they suspected we were after it, they would soon move it to another hiding-place or even pack it cross-country to the Nile and ship it out by the Mediterranean."

Frank and Harry asked leave to hold a brief consultation at the conclusion of which, they announced that they would think the matter over, and see Mr. Barr at his office the next day. The old man was far too shrewd to insist on a decision then and there, and so he left the hotel with the boys' promise to consider the matter carefully. As for Frank and Harry, they had pretty well made up their minds not to have anything to do with Mr. Barr, but an unforeseen circumstance altered their determination. As Barr left the room with Mr. Beasley, Lathrop turned on them with troubled eyes.

"Will you do it, Frank?" he asked anxiously. "Please say yes."

"Why, Lathrop, whatever is the matter," asked Harry,

noticing the almost painful anxiety, with which the boy looked at Frank and hung on his decision.

"It's just this," said the boy in a voice that shook, as he tried to steady it, "if that ivory isn't found, we shall be ruined. My father will be beggared."

"Beggared," exclaimed both the Boy Aviators who had regarded Mr. Beasley - as indeed did his friends in general - as one of the "best fixed" business men in New York.

"It's true,'" said Lathrop, despairingly. "He has been speculating foolishly and entered into an agreement with this man Barr to borrow money for still further stock deals. The only hope he has of paying his debts is the realization of the profits he could have made on the ivory. Its theft was a bitter blow to him, not so much for his own sake, as for my mother and sisters. Myself I don't care, I can get out and work, but it would break my heart to see them reduced to poverty."

The situation was a difficult one for the Chester Boys. They had taken a hearty dislike to the crafty old ivory merchant and had made up their minds not to enter into any enterprise in which he was interested. Here, however, was a new complication.

"Give us half-an-hour, Lathrop," said Frank at length, and the two boys withdrew to another room to talk the matter over. It was ten minutes past the agreed time when they came back.

In the meantime Lathrop had been joined by his father and the two had waited in painful anticipation for the Boy Aviators' verdict.

"Well - ," began Lathrop eagerly as the two boys with grave faces reentered the room.

"Well," said Frank, with a smile, "I guess we'll help you out, Lath."

Tears stood in the eyes of both Mr. Beasley and his son, as in shaky voices they endeavored to thank the Chester Boys.

"That's all right, Lathrop," said Frank at length - "turn about's fair play. You drove the aeroplane to Bellman's island you remember and saved us - now, we'll save you and your father, if we can - how long can you give us, Mr. Beasley?" he asked, briskly turning to the thoroughly humbled merchant.

"Eight weeks - if I hear from you by cable in eight weeks I can keep things going," was the reply.

"Phew!" whistled Frank, "that's not an awful lot of time."

"Can you do it, Frank?" asked Lathrop eagerly.

"We'll try as hard as we know how," was the modest answer.

"And - and you'll take me along?" faltered Lathrop.

"Sure, you can come as your father's representative at large," laughed Frank.

CHAPTER III

THE DARK CONTINENT

About a month after the events related in the last chapter the bluff-bowed French coasting steamer, Admiral Dupont, dropped anchor in the shallow roadstead off the steamy harbor of Fort Assini on the far-famed Ivory Coast. A few days before, the boys had left Sierra Leone and engaged quarters on the cockroach-infested little craft for the voyage down the coast. It was blisteringly hot and from off the shore there was borne on the wind the peculiar smell that every traveler knows as "African." It is the essence of the dark continent. Our young voyagers and Ben sniffed at it eagerly.

"Smells like marigolds," said Billy at last - and it did.

But there was soon plenty more to discuss than the strange appearance of the town, which in reality was little more than a big village with here and there one, or two houses of some pretension scattered about. For the rest, it consisted of the wickerwork huts of the natives. Back of the town were dense forests and beyond these again a long blue line of hills. An unhealthful looking lagoon lay between the houses and the mainland, into which the boys had been told the Bia River, up which they were to begin their voyage to the interior, emptied.

A broad yellow beach stretched in front of the houses and from this, as soon as the little steamer dropped anchor, whaleboats and canoes in great numbers were launched through what looked to be a thunderous surf. They were navigated by Kroomen - or Krooboys as they are sometimes called - and who are a superior race to most of the natives of Africa.

Some of the paddlers and oarsmen in the boats that surrounded the Admiral Dupont were almost six feet in height and splendidly built.

"Good looking fellows those," said the captain, who had joined the group of wondering young adventurers, "but in spite of their good looks they are petty thieves, if they get the chance."

Of this quality, the boys were soon to get an example. Frank had laid down his field-glasses on a deck chair and didn't give them any more thought, even when the decks were fairly swarming with half-naked, chattering, laughing Kroomen. When he looked around for them, however, for the purpose of making out more clearly the outline of the distant mountains, the glasses had vanished.

The young leader quickly divined what had occurred and stepping to the rail he held above his head an English sovereign and a pair of glasses, borrowed, from Billy.

"I'll give this money to the man who finds my field glasses," he shouted.

"It's a long chance," he remarked to Harry, "there may be some one there who understands English. Anyway they can see that I'm willing to give money for something like the object I held up."

As much to Frank's astonishment as anyone else the next minute they heard a hail from a canoe containing two particularly black Kroomen.

"Hey, boss;" one of them was shouting, "what you lost, eh?"

"Some one stole my field-glasses," shouted back Frank.

"All right, American massa," hailed back the Krooman, "I sail long time 'Merican ships. I catch him for you."

"Well, what do you think of that?" demanded Billy. "If the Statue of Liberty had come off her perch and done a song and dance you couldn't have astonished me more than to hear that sack of coal talk English."

"They take several of those fellows to sea on trading ships, that stop in here for logs from the interior," struck in Ben. "It wouldn't surprise me but what that fellow there has been in New York harbor, yes, and in San Francisco too."

The boys looked their astonishment.

"They are good hard workers," went on Ben, "and make good sailormen. They always come back here though in the end. They are as home loving as a house cat.'"

While the boys talked, their baggage was being hoisted into a lighter that lay alongside, ready for shipment ashore. They were about ready to quit the ship when their attention was attracted by a terrific uproar among the natives alongside. Two or three canoes had been upset and in the water half a dozen Kroomen were splashing about like big, black fish.

"They'll drown," gasped Harry, as he watched the furious water battle.

"Not them," sniffed Ben, "they are as much at home in the water as they are ashore. Hello!" he exclaimed, suddenly pointing, "there's your field-glasses again, Frank."

Sure enough, from the hands of a spluttering, half-drowned native, the Krooman who spoke English had just wrested a dripping pair of black morocco-covered field-glasses. He held them aloft in triumph, treading water while he held the other's head under the sea as a punishment for his thievery.

"I catch 'um, boss, I catch um," he kept shouting triumphantly. A few seconds later, having half drowned the unfortunate thief, he stood dripping like a figure cut out of black basalt before the boy. As he received his recovered property Frank presented its rescuer with the sovereign. If it had been a fortune the man could not have been more overcome with gratitude. He sank on his knees.

"You come ashore my boat?" he begged. "Cost nothing to United States boys."

The adventurers assented and, having seen their

baggage properly stowed on the lighter, they landed through the surf a short time later and found themselves on the flat, yellow beach facing the rather dreary looking row of Europeans' houses. The method of landing the surf boats and the wonderful dexterity with which the natives handle them is worth a whole chapter to itself. But it might prove tedious reading, so suffice it to say, that with one man standing erect in the stern with a steering oar, and the others paddling like demons, the Ivory Coast boatmen invariably land their passengers, in a smother of foam which seems overwhelming, without spilling a drop of water on them. Not a visitor to this coast but has been impressed by their wonderful skill.

"Well, here we are," remarked Billy, looking about him at the novel surroundings.

"The first thing to do," announced Frank, "is to go to the house of Monsieur Desplaines, to whom Mr. Barr gave us a letter of introduction, and talk over our plans."

Monsieur Desplaines was the consular agent of the United States government at Assini, which is a French port, and had promised by cable to Mr. Barr to give, the young travelers all the advice that his experiences could suggest. He had also volunteered to select for them a train of native baggage carriers, and hunters that would be reliable. There are no roads into the heart of Africa and everything is transported by human pack-trains. The natives of this part of the coast are strong, muscular men not easily fatigued and are capable of carrying burdens on their heads twenty-five miles or more a day without exhaustion.

As the boys started to make their way up the beach a trim figure with neatly waxed black mustaches, almost extinguished in a huge pith helmet and dressed in white duck with a red sash about the waist, emerged from the nearest house and hastened toward them.

"Welcome to Africa!" cried the newcomer as he approached and who, as Frank at once guessed, was M. Desplaines himself. "Come with me to the house and make yourselves at home."

The boys shook hands warmly with the little Frenchman who seemed so hospitably inclined and followed him eagerly toward the whitewashed house from which be had emerged.

"I would have been at the steamer to meet you," he exclaimed apologetically; "but she got here a day ahead of time and I was not prepared."

Inside the house, which was delightfully cool and darkened by jalousies from the glaring heat outside, the young adventurers were introduced to Madame Desplaines and two little girls, who constituted the family of the consular agent, who also kept the general supply store at Assini.

After dinner that evening, M. Desplaines talked long and earnestly to the boys. Of the real object of their mission, he had of course no knowledge. That was kept a secret even from Barr's intimates. There was too much at stake to let it leak out. His idea was the boys had come on a hunting and exploration, much of which was to be performed by aeroplane. He informed the boys that, acting on cabled instructions, he had laid in a good supply of gasoline by the last steamer from

Sierra Leone and that arrangements for a train of carriers and for boats up the river had been made. There was a wheezy steam launch belonging to the trading post which would tow the boats up the Bia River as far as they desired. The Kroomen the boys engaged would take them to that point would then be abandoned, as they refused to go far from the coast. Such was the outline of M. Desplaines' conversation with the travelers.

The evening was far advanced when already the little party was ready for bed and already their imaginations had been fired by the tales that the consular agent had told them of the interior of the wild Bambara country. As they were saying good night to their hospitable host and hostess, there was a knock at the door. In response to M. Desplaines shouted: "Come in," a tall coal-black figure stalked into the lamp-light. The glow shone warmly on his black skin and lit up the mighty muscles that played beneath it. The strength of the man was evidently tremendous. The boys, to their surprise, recognized him at once, as the rescuer of Frank's opera-glasses. He paid no attention to Desplaines or his family, but walked straight up to Frank.

"Hi boss, you go hunt, you go far into land of Bambara," he said, raising his mighty arm and pointing to the northeast.

Frank nodded.

It was a strange scene. The boys and Ben in their hunting costumes and stout boots, M. Desplaines, short and inclined to be fat and as neatly barbered and tailored as if he had just stepped off the boulevards, Madame Desplaines and her little girls in cool, white frocks - and in the center of the group - dominating it by his impressive manner and mighty form - the huge, ebony Krooman.

"In the land of Bambara much game," went on the Krooman.

"So we have heard," replied Frank.

"In the land of Bambara much danger," continued the Krooman, fixing his dark eyes full on Frank, "much danger to the white boys, who fly like birds."

"Why, how do you know that?" exclaimed Frank, amazed that the Krooman should not only know their destination - which might have been a guess - but have divined the fact that they had an aeroplane.

"Krooman know much that white man not know!" replied the giant black.

Then, rising his finger, he counted the amazed group of adventurers who stood transfixed at the scene.

"One - two - three - four - five go to Bambara," he intoned. "Come back one - two - three. Two die. Sikaso, know."

Before any of the astounded party could frame a question or open their lips, the huge figure had stalked to the doorway and vanished.

"He'd make a nice, comfortable house-pet that fellow," said Billy, who was the first to speak. "One, two, three, four, five go to Bambara," he mimicked. "Come back one, two, three. Two die. Sikaso know. Br-r-r-r-r, he gives me the creeps."

They all laughed at Billy's absurd aping of the stately negro, but nevertheless none of them felt inclined for more talk that night. Somehow, the Krooman had cast a gloom on the party. Had they known how nearly his prophecy was to come to fulfillment they might even have been tempted to abandon the expedition.

CHAPTER IV

THE WITCH-DOCTOR

Bright and early the next day Frank and Harry were up and stirring, and the other members of the party were not long in joining them. The almost innumerable packing cases and chests containing the duffle, ammunition, armament and the sections of the Golden Eagle were scattered about the little "compound" or garden of M. Desplaines' residence, having been brought ashore overnight by a crew of Kroomen. M. Desplaines appeared while the boys were still contemplating their outfit and wondering if it would be possible to accommodate it all in the little flotilla which, it had been arranged previously, was to take them up the river to the camping place from which they were to strike out for the Ivory Mountain.

"I really almost envy your trip," he said, "although it will be fraught with danger. Still you go well armed and provisioned, and from what I have heard of you, you are not the sort of boys to let a few obstacles upset you."

While they were still talking and waiting for breakfast to be announced they were joined by a singular figure. It was that of a white man in rather shabby ducks and crowned, as was M. Desplaines, with a huge, white pith helmet. Over one shoulder he carried a green butterfly net and under one arm he had tucked a tin box. Round his waist was a leather belt from which hung, in addition to a revolver and cartridges, a glass bottle with a wide stopper with a chloroformed sponge reposing in the bottom. It did not need the introduction of the newcomer by M. Desplaines as Professor Ajax Wiseman, to tell the boys that Dr. Wiseman was a naturalist.

"My dear professor, what are you doing here?" exclaimed M. Desplaines as soon as the introductions were over.

"I arrived this morning from Grand Bassam on a coasting schooner," replied the professor, carefully setting down his tin box. "I have a remarkable specimen of the Gladiolus Gorgeosi in there," he remarked importantly. "I am contemplating a trip into the interior via the Bia River and came to you to see if you could arrange transportation."

M. Desplaines looked at the boys.

"These young men have engaged the steam launch, to tow their expedition up the river," he said hesitatingly; "they are going on a hunting trip, into the interior, and have, I venture to say, one of the most complete outfits I have ever seen."

The naturalist looked wistfully at Frank.

"I suppose there would not be the least objection to my availing myself of your assistance in getting up the river," he said, blinking behind his spectacles like an old bat who has unexpectedly emerged into the sunlight. "I have only two canoes and as I carry my own attendant I shall be no trouble."

"We shall be delighted to accommodate you," rejoined Frank heartily, "but I shall have to place one restriction on you. When we reach our destination we must part company as we have work to do of a confidential nature. Our employer, Mr. Barr - "

"Old Luther Barr," burst out Professor Wiseman suddenly.

"Why, yes," rejoined Frank, rather taken aback, "you know him then?"

"I - I have heard of him," replied the other with a slight hesitancy which was, however, so faint as to be hardly noticeable. The voice of Madame Desplaines summoning them to breakfast broke off any opportunity for further questions on a matter that plainly, for some strange reason or other, seemed to have heartily interested - even disturbed - the naturalist. Frank felt troubled for a moment at the idea of having let Professor Wiseman form a portion of their party even for a short distance. But he dismissed the idea almost instantly. The queer expression that passed over Professor Wiseman's face at the mention of the ivory trader's name might have simply been due to astonishment at hearing it again. Still Frank decided to keep an eye on Professor Wiseman.

The conversation at breakfast naturally enough dealt with the little known country the boys were to penetrate. Then it was for the first time that they heard mention of the mysterious tribe of the Flying Men who were reported to be equipped with rudimentary wings

- like those of an undeveloped bat with which they managed to flit from tree top to tree top like true flyers.

"Oh, come," laughed Billy, "I've heard of tailed men and white Africans with red top-knots like Lathrop, but a race of winged men is coming it too strong."

"Laugh if you like," declared Professor Wiseman who had brought up the subject, "but some time ago I articulated a skeleton brought me by an Arab slave trader and found extending from the shoulder blade two distinct bony frames which had in life apparently been covered with a thin fleshy substance of leathery like tenacity stretching thence to the wrists. I asked the slave trader where he had found the skeleton," went on the savant, "and he told me he had come across it at the foot of a giant silk cotton tree in the Bambara country."

The boys exchanged glances. It was to the Bambara country - the country of the legendary Flying Men - that they were bound.

"Is any more known of this tribe?" inquired Frank.

"Very little except what you can pick up from the natives, which is little enough," replied Professor Wiseman, "they seem to have a dislike to speaking of the Flying Men - to whites at any rate. I think, too, they fear them. Report has it that they live in cave-like holes in the side of a giant, black basalt cliff reached by a subterranean river. They reach the ground by taking short flights from the holes they live in and regain the cliff dwellings by means of rope ladders formed of twisted creepers."

"Then they cannot fly upward?" asked Frank.

"It would seem not," replied the naturalist, "their wings only serve as gliders. Possibly once in the remote ages they could fly as well as great birds but with the course of the ages and disuse their wings have dwindled."

As may, be imagined the idea that within a short time they were to be in the country of the mysterious tribe caused a tremendous stir among the boys and when after breakfast their strange friend of the night before, Sikaso, appeared they at once overwhelmed him with questions. But strangely enough Sikaso made no reply to their eager queries.

He shook his great bead and seemed to be embarrassed, if not by fear at any rate by reticence.

"In Misoto Mountains many strange Ju-jus (fetishes)," he said in an awed tone, "Misoto Mountains no good for white boys - white boys stay away."

"Not much," chimed in Harry, "that's just where we are going."

"You go Misoto Mountain," said the giant black in an astonished tone.

"That's what we are," exclaimed Lathrop.

The black gazed at the ground and drew a small circle on the dust with his toe. In the center of it he made a cross.

"That my dukkeri (fate)," he said slowly, "you go, Sikaso he go too. I see it in the smoke."

"Saw it in the smoke?" repeated the amazed boys.

"In smoke of Ju-ju fire I see it written. I see five go, three come back, in smoke too. I have spoken."

He stalked off as I suddenly as he had the night before and left the boys to gaze in a bewildered way after his huge figure as it swung down the road.

"That fellow's the best disappearer I ever saw," said Billy Barnes at length.

"I wish he'd stop that stuff about 'five go three come back,'" said Lathrop, "it gets on your nerves."

"What could he have meant by seeing it in the smoke?" asked Harry bewilderedly.

"Just this," broke in a quiet voice behind them. It was Professor Wiseman, who had glided up to them as silently as a cat. "It is a common trick among the witch doctors - of whom our friend yonder seems to be one - to divine events by means of the smoke from a fire built to the accompaniment of special incantations."

"Well, that's cheerful," commented Billy, "but tell us, Professor, how often do they hit it right?"

"Nine times out of ten, young man," said Professor Wiseman impressively fixing Billy with his gaze just as he would have impaled a bug or grasshopper, "and the tenth time they come so near the truth as to be uncomfortable."

"I have heard of such things, but I always put them down as impossibilities," gasped Frank.

"Just travelers' tales," said Billy.

"There are many things for the young to learn in Africa," remarked Professor Wiseman coldly and gazing at Billy with squashing intentness; "the young do not believe many things merely because they are young - and foolish."

"Gee! that was a nailer for fair," said Billy afterward. "I felt as if the Doc was running a big blue pin through me and sticking me on a bit of cork,"

That morning, as the start for the interior was not to be made till the next day, M. Desplaines asked the boys if they would care to try a little fishing at the foot of the famous Jumbari Falls which lay on a branch of the Bari river a short distance from the town. Of course the boys assented eagerly, but as it was found that only Frank and Harry were expert canoeists, it was agreed that the others should fish from the bank while the two young leaders trolled their lines from a native built craft. This canoe was kept at the falls - to which they tramped the two miles overland by a narrow trail.

The falls were a magnificent sight. From a dark red rock, fully two hundred feet in height, a great volume of water poured its roaring current into a boiling pool below. The cliffs shot up sheer on all sides and were covered at the bottom with luxuriant green growth like seaweed, while higher up, ferns, as big as rose-bushes at home, and trees of a hundred varieties clung wherever they could find a root-hold. As the party arrived at the top of the ravine and gazed down, the uproar of the water was so terrific as to render any speech inaudible. M. Desplaines, who led the party, pointed to a hole in the rocks and a second later vanished into it.

At first, consternation seized on the boys who thought that an accident had happened, but seeing not hearing Professor Wiseman's reassuring laugh and noticing him plunge after M. Desplaines, the boys rightly concluded that the aperture was a subterranean entrance to the foot of the falls. And so it proved. A steep flight of steps was cut in a deep cleft of the cliff down to the water's edge. A few minutes after they had begun the descent, the little party stood on the brink of the whirling pool into which the mighty falls roared their thousands of tons of water. Following M. Desplaines, they advanced down the stream to a point where a bend shut off like a rock curtain the deafening uproar of the cascade. Here a canoe lay moored and Frank and Harry stepped into it and shoved off. Their lines and other equipment they had in their pockets.

As they shoved out M. Desplaines shouted something that they did not catch and pointed down the stream. How near the fact that they could not hear his words was to come to costing them their lives neither of the boys guessed.

CHAPTER V

THE POOL OF DEATH

"Say, Frank, have you noticed that we are going to have a hard paddle back against this current?"

The boys had been fishing about an hour when Harry spoke. So engrossed had they both been pulling in fish of a dozen strange varieties and brilliant hues that neither of the lads had noticed that the canoe had drifted down stream far from the starting point and that in fact when they looked up they were in an entirely strange part of the river.

"You are right, Harry," rejoined Frank, as he looked up at the steep banks on either side of them, "we have drifted a considerable distance. Come on, out with the paddles and we'll be getting back."

But it was one thing to talk of getting back and quite another thing to do it. The boys, after an hour of paddling, were dismayed to find that although their arms ached with the exertion and they were dripping with perspiration, they had made hardly any progress against the current.

"It's too much for us," gasped Frank.

"What on earth are we going to do?" asked Harry with blanched cheeks.

Frank glanced at the shore on either side. For a minute he had entertained a thought of landing and walking back along the beach. But there was no beach.

The river boiled along between narrow walls which shot sheer up from the water. There was not even a niche in their smooth surface to afford a foothold to a mountain goat. They were caught in a trap.

The only thing to do was to drift down the river and trust to luck to find a landing-place. In their extremity they shouted at the top of their voices to let their comrades know of their plight, but their cries were unanswered and they began to wish that they had saved their breath to use in the task of keeping the canoe steady in the current.

While they had been pondering their situation, moreover, they had been swept with almost incredible rapidity down the river. The walls here grew narrower and narrower and the water fairly boiled in its narrow confines. Its dark surface was flecked with white foam, and to make matters worse, as the walls closed in the light became fainter, till the boys were being carried downward through almost subterranean darkness.

In the intense gloom their white strained faces shone out like pallid beacon-lights.

"Hold her steady," said Frank in a tense voice as the canoe wobbled crazily in the swollen current.

"I'm doing the best I can," gasped out poor Harry

desperately plying his paddle.

It the canoe was to get broadside onto the current, even for the fraction of a second, Frank well knew that nothing could save them. It was a terrible situation.

Helplessly they were being borne at dizzy speed to what seemed almost certain death - for certain it was that they could not hold out much longer. Already their overstrained muscles were only mechanically doing their duty, but before long Frank realized that even his-well-trained young body must collapse - and then, what?

Suddenly there was borne to their ears a sound that made both boys chill with terror.

It was a mighty roaring like the furious boiling of some giant kettle. A thousand shouting voices seemed blended into one to form the music, of this ominous orchestra. Louder the noise grew and louder, as the pass through which the river now tore like a runaway race-horse grew narrower and blacker.

What could the awful uproar mean?

They had not long to wait before the truth burst upon them. They were nearing, at what seemed express speed, a whirling, roaring mass of waters that shouted at them like some animal calling for its prey. The boys' cheeks blanched as they realized that nothing but a miracle could save them from being sucked into this watery abyss.

Desperately they plied their paddles but if they had been useless further up the stream they were doubly inefficient now. If they had stroked against the rushing current with feathers they could not have had less effect in checking the death rush of the canoe, which was tossed along on the racing tide like a chip of wood.

Suddenly the canoe was struck a terrific blow.

Before either boy could realize what had happened they were both struggling in the water. So dazed were they by the mishap that it was several minutes before they understood that they were clinging to the to the trunk of some huge tree. It was this trunk that had wrecked the canoe and thrown them overboard.

In reality, though, they were little better off now than they had been while the canoe was being whirled down the river. It looked as if they had been saved from one death only to face a worse. With all their might they clung side by side. Dripping wet, half-blinded and bruised by the battering they got as the trunk smashed from side to side of the narrow passage, the indomitable American pluck of the two lads yet held good in this extremity.

"Is it good-by, Frank?" Harry found strength to murmur.

"While there's life there's hope," came Frank's brave reply in his favorite axiom. "We'll live to fly the old Golden Eagle yet, let's hope."

There was no time for further talk, even had the boys been in any position to consider conversation. The trunk was rapidly nearing the whirlpool - and death.

Small wonder that brave as the boys were a despairing cry burst from their throats as they saw what seemed the end of their ride close upon them. It was as if they could feel the breath of the Pale Horseman already blowing chilly in their faces.

But suddenly a strange thing happened.

Both boys had closed their eyes and only moved their lips in prayer as they saw that inevitably in a few minutes they must be sucked into the maelstrom. Now, however, they opened them in amazement.

The swift rush of the log to which they clung like drowned rats had stopped.

It took them only a few seconds to take in what had occurred. The great log swinging one end toward the swirling current had jammed clear across the stream and for a time at any rate they were saved from immediate death. In their joy they clasped each other's hands warmly but their first rush of relief did not last long. As a matter of fact they were not any nearer safely than they had been a few minutes previous.

The log, it was true, was jammed across the stream, but the consequent backing up of the impetuous current caused it to rush across the boys' refuge in such volumes as to almost sweep them from their perches.

It was very evident that they could not hold put indefinitely in this position.

Their attention was attracted as they clung to their water-swept tree-trunk by a dark object whirling about in the boiling pool. It was swept dizzily round and round in ever decreasing circles toward the middle of the fatal vortex. Suddenly it shot downward out of sight, but as it did so Frank had seen something that kindled one ray of hope - though a feeble one. Before the canoe had taken the fatal downward plunge it had hesitated for a minute as though caught on something; and then the boy leader saw for the first time that in the center of the pool there was a rock, although the water that submerged it to the depth of an inch or so prevented its being seen at first glance.

Frank turned to Harry and told him of his discovery.

"If we are cast into the pool let us make up our minds to get to that rock. Keep your mind concentrated on it. Don't let the idea leave you for a second and perhaps - I say 'perhaps' - we can make it."

Harry shook his head despairingly.

"I can hardly keep my grip on this tree. I don't believe that I could possibly manage to swim even a few yards," he groaned.

"You must," said Frank sharply. "Don't give in now, Harry. Stick it out."

Then as a sudden thought struck him he continued.

"See here, it's no good our wasting our strength clinging to this trunk any longer. Sooner or later we shall be swept off and the longer we wait the less reserve strength we shall have. Let us leave go now and swim for it."

Whatever reply Harry might have tendered to this

desperate proposal he was spared making, for at that moment a wave of more than ordinary force - caused by the backed-up water striking the log - struck him full in the face and before he knew it the boy had been washed from the tree trunk and was being carried like a straw down the stream.

As Harry felt himself being carried along there was only one thought in his mind. It was not of death. When death is right upon a man or a boy he rarely thinks of it, but casts about for the best means of saving himself. Nor does - as some imaginative writers have told us - a man's whole past life come before him at such moments. No - the instinct of self-preservation is strongest when a human being is in the direst need, and so it was that in Harry's mind one thought kept hammering away like the strokes of a tolling bell.

"Try-and-make-the-rock. Try-and-make-the-rock."

Frank's insistence had done this much. It had caused the boy to recollect the one hope of salvation that the desperate situation held out. As he was swept down the torrent Harry made no effort to swim. It would have been worse than useless and besides he needed to husband his strength for the final struggle he knew was upon him.

The next minute he felt a sickening swirling sensation and realized that he was in the whirlpool's death-grip at last.

Faster and faster the boy was hurried in ever decreasing circles. Dizzy, half-choked with water, blinded and almost exhausted Harry, with the tenacity of a bull dog, still clung tenaciously to the one idea:

"Try-and-make-the-rock. Try-and-make-the-rock."

Suddenly, he was flung against a hard substance. With outstretched fingers he clutched at the slimy surface as of what he realized was the end of his journey at last. The great stone was covered with slimy weed, however, and his grasping fingers refused to clutch at any friendly niche in its surface.

With a despairing cry the boy was being swept in to the terrible mouth of the pool when he felt himself seized and pulled up out of the grip of the torrent. He knew no more till he opened his eyes and found Frank by his side. Both boys were on the rock - sitting on it in two inches or more of water. Fortunately in that climate the water was not so chilly as to cause discomfort, but this was about the only crumb of satisfaction the situation held for them.

"Well done, old fellow," said Frank as Harry opened his eyes. "You had a narrow escape, though."

Harry could only look at his brother gratefully. How deep was his debt of gratitude to him both boys realized without their talking of it.

"How did you gain the rock, Frank?" asked Harry.

"When I saw you swept off the tree trunk I slipped off too," replied Frank, "and when I felt myself dragged into the pool I struck out for the rock. I confess, though, I didn't have much hope of reaching it till I was slammed into it with a blow that almost cracked my ribs and knocked all the wind out of me. I managed however to grab hold of a depression in the surface and maintain my grip on it. I had hardly dragged myself up when you were hurled against it. I thought I had lost you, for the water pulled like a draught-horse, but I managed to hold on to you and here we are."

"And a worse position we could not possibly be in," added Harry.

"Unless we were in there," retorted Frank pointing, not without a shudder, to the whirling open mouth of the pool which had sucked down the wreck of their canoe.

"What is it do you suppose?" asked Harry wonderingly.

"The mouth of a subterranean river I guess," replied Frank. "I have read of such things."

"But why didn't Desplaines warn us of our danger," said Harry bitterly, "if we ever get out of this I shall tell him my opinion of him pretty strongly. We might have been killed and we may yet."

"He did warn us," replied Frank calmly.

"He did?"

"Yes."

"I should like to know when?"

"When we shoved off."

"You mean when he shouted something we couldn't catch and pointed down the river?"

"That's it."

"I thought he meant there was better fishing down, here," snapped Harry indignantly, "what idiots we were."

"Yes; not to notice how we were drifting," rejoined Frank quietly, "it's no use to blame Mr. Desplaines for this pickle. We have only ourselves to be angry with. I don't suppose he ever thought that two boys would not notice how they were drifting in a ten mile current."

"The point is how are we ever going to get out of it?"

How indeed?

As the boys looked about they saw little to encourage them. The chasm in which they were beleaguered was not more than fifteen feet across, but on either side shot up walls of rock so steep and smooth that not even a fern could find root on their polished surfaces.

Where the whirlpool sank into the bowels of the earth the walls came together at an angle forming a sort of triangular prison. At the top of this trap the boys could see a strip of blue sky and the outlines of the graceful tops of some bulbous stemmed palms but nothing else. Once a vulture sailed across the strip and sighting the two boys came lower to investigate. The sight of the carrion bird made both of the boys shudder.

"Ugh, he scents a meal, he thinks we're dead already," cried Harry disgustedly.

The sound of his voice echoed gloomily among the rocks.

"We're dead already," came back in sepulchral tones.

"I shan't try to wake that echo up again," said Harry in a low tone and shivering at the uncanny voice of the rock.

Neither of the boys spoke for a long time. They sat there silently, occasionally standing up to get the stiffness out of their limbs till the strip of sky above began to darken to gray.

"Well, here goes!" exclaimed Harry suddenly.

Frank glanced sharply up. He did not like the wild tone in which the words were spoken.

"What is it?" he asked sharply.

"I'm tired of this, I'm going to swim for it," replied Harry with a foolish, hysterical laugh.

Frank saw what had happened. The boy had become half-delirious under the mental strain he had undergone.

"Sit down, old fellow," he said kindly, "help will come soon I am sure."

"Yes, a steamboat will come sailing down the river and take us home in the captain's cabin I suppose," said Harry foolishly.

But nevertheless Frank's stern command to "shut up" and not make a foot of himself brought him to his senses and he said no more till the stillness was broken by a sudden cry from above.

"Bosses - oh, bosses."

"Ahoy there; castaways!"

Frank looked up.

The cry of joy he gave set the echoes flying in the gloomy canyon.

It was the black face of Sikaso that was gazing down on them and beside it was Ben Stubbs' weather-beaten countenance. Behind them were Billy, Lathrop and the rest.

"Hold on there and we'll get you out of that in two shakes of a duck's tail," cheerily hailed the old adventurer. "We guessed you'd be here and we brought a rope as long as a man of war's cable with us. Lucky thing we did."

The next minute a long rope of vegetable fiber came snaking down the side of the cliff and to one end of it clung Ben Stubbs. As he reached the bottom - the rope being cautiously paid out from above by his companions - the old seaman swung himself outward from the face of the rock and "in a brace of shakes," as he would have said, stood alongside the two boys. In a second his sharp eye took in Harry's wild looks and hysterical greetings and realized what had happened.

"Now, Frank," he ordered, giving the young aviator the end of the rope - "catch hold tight and when you are ready give the word."

"But Harry - " gasped Frank, "I can't leave him. Let him go first."

"I'll bring him up. He can't look after himself in the

shape he's in and you are too weak to attempt to help him. Now no talking back. I'm boss now. Up aloft with you. Haul away there!"

The next minute Frank, clinging to the rope, was being hauled cautiously up the side of the sheer cliff by careful hands and shortly he was in the arms of his friends.

Ben Stubbs - to whom the rope with a weight at the end of it had been swung pendulum wise - next appeared at the summit with Harry in his strong grip. But it was a white faced inanimate burden he carried. The boy had swooned.

"He'll be all right in a few minutes," said Ben Stubbs as M. Desplaines and the others all tried to explain at once to Frank how Sikaso had guessed what had happened when the boys did not return. The Krooman had led the party by secret native trails to the cliff top. Frank clasped the huge black's hand with real gratitude and tears of thankfulness brimmed in his eyes.

"How can I ever thank you," he said.

"Um - white boys keep away Pool of Death, Sikaso much pleased," replied the Krooman turning slowly away with a sad expression on his face.

"His own son was drowned in it several years ago," said M. Desplaines briefly.

CHAPTER VI

A SNAP-SHOT FIEND IN TROUBLE

The morning after the events recorded in the last chapter was one of these sparkling ones that are occasionally to be met with on the West African coast and was the forerunner of a day of great bustle and activity for the boys. With the vitality of healthy youth Harry had completely recovered and was indeed surprised to find himself feeling so good after what he had been through. Privately he inspected his hair in the mirror to see if it had turned white and was secretly much astonished to find it the same color as before.

"I wish mine would turn white or potato color or something," said Lathrop, to whom Harry confided his expectation, "this red thatch of mine is a nuisance. At school I was always Brick-top or Red-Head and out here the natives all look at my carrot-colored top-knot as if they'd like to scalp me and keep it for a fetish."

Both boys laughed heartily over Lathrop's half-assumed vexation. As a matter of fact he had been the butt of many jokes in school on account of his blazing red hair and in Africa the natives with their love for any gaudy color had already christened him Rwome Mogo or Red-Top. Of this, however, he was fortunately ignorant, as he might have been tempted to go out and dispatch half a dozen of them if he knew of their term for him.

Down at the river bank, cross the evil-smelling lagoon at the back of the town, Frank and Harry had their hands full directing shouting, laughing Kroomen how to load up the canoes. From the canopied steam launch that lay alongside the rickety wharf the black engineer - an American Negro - watched with great contempt their labors, which they enlivened with songs from time to time.

"Them's de mos' good fur nuffingest niggahs I ever did see," remarked Mr. Rastus Johnson - that was his name - with undisguised contempt.

Nevertheless by noon the canoes had all been leaded and the farewells to the kind M. Desplaines and his family said. After a swift final inspection Frank pronounced everything ship-shape and even Doctor Wiseman who had been fussing about as Billy said "like a hen with one chicken - and that a lame duck," over his tin cases and poisonous looking bottles, announced that he was ready to start. The twelve chattering Kroomen who were to go as far as the Bambara country with the expedition were seated two in each canoe. They were along simply as camp attendants and packers and would by no means go any further than the borders of the Bambara country which they said was the dwelling-place of "bery bad man sah."

Just as the little launch, flying the stars and stripes out of compliment to the boys, was drawing out into the stream with a long blast of her whistle, a tall, black form came racing along the bank and with one bound cleared the five feet or so between the launch and the shore. It was Sikaso.

"So you came after all," said Frank, turning to him, after a bend in the, river had hidden the waving Mr. Desplaines from sight and they were settling down in the launch.

"Sikaso see in the smoke I come - I come. If I see in smoke I no come - I no come," remarked the Krooman.

"He's traveling light anyhow," remarked Billy.

Indeed the giant negro's only bit of baggage was a huge axe, the handle of which was dented and scarred as if by many combats. Billy was about to run his thumb along its edge when with a gesture the mighty negro waved him aside. Instead he took Billy's handkerchief from the young reporter's pocket and drew it gently along the axe blade.

It fell in two pieces on each side of his blade, severed by its razor-like edge.

"Sikaso is a good fellow to be friends with when he can make little ones out of big ones like that," remarked Billy, picking up the two fragments of his handkerchief, "that's a fine way to cut up a gentleman's wardrobe."

Bit by bit as the launch drove steadily up the muddy river - from whose jungle-grown banks arose a warm, moist vapor - Frank drew from the grim-faced old Krooman some of his history. He had been a mighty warrior in the old days, he said, and the weapon be carried was his war axe with which he had killed uncounted enemies. A rival tribe, however, had killed his father and mother and driven him to the coast with the few survivors of his village. Here he had shipped on an American trading brig for New York where he had picked up the knowledge of English he possessed. He also worshiped America as "free man's country." But Africa had called to him and some three years before he had returned on another ship and meant to die there, he said.

"Why did you wish to go with us?" asked Frank as the native concluded his story.

"It was written so in the smoke, white boss," replied the veteran simply. "The ju-ju in the smoke strong ju-ju. He knows many things."

"Is that the only reason you have for coming?"

"No, boss, I tell you truth," replied the old warrior, "some day I find the chief who kill my father and my mother and kill my friends." He glanced significantly at his axe.

"In the Moon Mountains maybe I find him - maybe not. But some day I shall and then - "

He said no more, but as Frank remarked to Harry when the former recounted his conversation to his brother later:

"I shouldn't much like to be that man when Sikaso meets him."

The launch and the small flotilla she towed forged steadily up the stream all that day and at nightfall drew alongside the bank at a spot where a clearing planted with bananas clearly indicated the presence thereabouts of a native village. As soon as the launch was moored to the bank the adventurers scrambled out - not sorry of a chance to stretch their legs - and looked about them wonderingly. They were really in equatorial Africa at last, and even as they looked there was a sound borne to their ears that brought home to them strongly how very far away they were from old New York. It was a pulsing, rhythmic beating something like a drum and yet unlike it. They looked questioningly at Sikaso.

"Tom-tom," said he briefly.

"Is it a friendly village, Sikaso?" inquired Doctor Wiseman.

"Friendly to some - not to all," replied the Krooman, who for some unaccountable reason had taken a strange dislike to the professor. "Come," he said, intoning to Frank and Harry, "we go see get chicken, maybe pork."

"Say, can't we come along, Frank?" asked Billy and Lathrop their faces falling.

Frank consulted Sikaso who merely said:

"Little fat white boy, with round, glass four-eyes talk too much."

"Well," laughed Frank, "I think I can promise for him that he won't do any talking that will cause any harm this evening."

"Talk too much, indeed," grumbled Billy highly offended, "why at home my folks were thinking of having a doctor treat me for bashfulness I'm so retiring in my disposition."

As soon as the laugh that this remark of the disgruntled reporter had caused had subsided - even old Sikaso giving a grim smile as he took in the purport of it - the little party set out down a native trail toward the village.

As the tom-tom beating increased in loudness as the village drew near, the boys' hearts began to beat a little faster. At last they were about to see a real African village - such as they had read about in Stanley's and Livingstone's books - and other less authentic volumes. They almost stumbled on the place as they suddenly emerged into a clearing. It was a strange sight that met their eyes.

Arranged in a circle were fifty huts that resembled nothing so much as a collection of old-fashioned straw covered beehives, enlarged to shelter human bees. All about them women and children were bustling; setting about getting the evening meal. Before one hut sat a woman, pounding something in a stone pestle - "like the drugstore men use at home," - whispered Lathrop to Billy.

The arrival of the little band created a stir. The hideous old man, with a sort of straw-bonnet, who had been beating on the antelope skin drum called by Sikaso a "tom-tom" saw them and instantly picked up his instrument and waddled off with as much dignity as his age and a much distended stomach would allow him. The younger men, however, advanced boldly toward the party. Some of them carried, spears, others held Birmingham matchlocks of the kind the British and French Governments have in vain tried to keep out of the hands of the West African natives. These guns are smuggled in by hundreds, by Arab traders who exchange the "gas-pipe" weapons worth perhaps two dollars a-piece for priceless ivory, and even human flesh for the slave dhows.

"Seesanah (peace)," said Sikaso gravely, advancing in his turn.

"Seesanah," echoed the tribesmen, who evidently recognized Sikaso from their greetings. The boys stood grouped in the background - Billy Barnes and Lathrop even viewing with some alarm the advance of the savage-looking natives.

"Well, he seems to have fallen in with several members of his club," remarked the irrepressible Billy as old Sikaso and the natives talked away at a great rate.

"I'm going to get a picture of some of these niggers when they get through," he continued aside to Lathrop.

"What; you brought a camera?" asked the other boy.

"Sure thing," replied Billy, "and if their ugly mugs don't break the lens, I mean to get some good snaps."

He drew a small flat folding camera from his pocket as he spoke and got it ready for action.

"Do you think Frank would stand for it? It might make trouble you know," said Lathrop.

"Pshaw," retorted the cocksure Billy, "what trouble can it make? I wish I knew bow to say 'Look pleasant, please,' in Hottentot, or whatever language these fellows talk."

By this time old Sikaso's 'pow-wow' was over and he motioned Frank and Harry forward. After they had been introduced to the chiefs and headmen of the village, the "big chief," a villainous-looking old party with only one eye and his legs thrust into a red shirt – into the armholes that is, with the rest of the garment rolled round his waist - announced he was ready to give fresh provisions for calico, red and blue, and several sections of the brass rod that passes for currency on the West Coast. While Frank, Harry and Sikaso were bargaining behind a hut, over the price to be charged for a razor-backed porker of suspicious appearance the village suddenly became filled with an uproar of angry shouts and tumult.

"What can be the matter?" exclaimed Frank, as the boys, followed by the old chief and Sikaso, rushed from behind the hut to ascertain the cause of the disturbance.

Standing in the center of a crowd of excited villagers was Billy Barnes, his helmet knocked off and an arrow sticking through it. He looked scared to death as well he might, for by his side was a stalwart young African, brandishing a heavy-bladed spear above his head. At the young reporter's feet lay the ill-fated camera that had caused all the trouble.

What had happened was this. As soon as Frank and Harry and their companions had left him and Lathrop alone, Billy had started to carry out his determination to take some pictures. The first subject he selected was a serious-faced little baby, innocent of any clothing, that sat playing with a ragged dog at, the entrance of one of the beehive huts. He had just clicked the button and exclaimed:

"This will be a jim-dandy," when he felt something whistle through the air and the next minute his hat lay at his feet with an arrow in it. In an instant the child's father - convinced that Billy was putting Ju-ju medicine on the child - was upon him, armed with his big hunting spear and followed by half the village. Even Billy - scared as he was - did not realize how very near to death he actually came to being. Sikaso's shouted words in a native dialect caused the tribesmen to fall back but they still muttered angrily.

Stepping swiftly up to the camera Sikaso with a single blow of his axe smashed it to pieces.

"Here, that's no way to treat my camera!" Billy was indignantly beginning, when Frank gripped his shoulder in an iron-clutch and whispered:

"Shut up; if you don't want to make more trouble."

Billy was starting on an angry remonstrance when he caught Frank's eye. The young leader was really angry and Billy prudently refrained from saying any more.

As for Sikaso - after demolishing Billy's machine, he turned to the tribesmen and addressing them in stately tones said - as he afterward translated it to Frank:

"Village fools. You see there is no magic in the little black box. It is nothing but a child's plaything for the fat, spectacled idiot." (This part of the oration Frank did not communicate to Billy.) "You see I have smashed it. Do I fear? Do I look now like a man in terror of the white man's medicine. It is nothing. It is broken and gone like the cloud before the wind, like the shadow on the mountain side."

The effect of all this was soothing and the boys left the camp, to order some of their packmen to bring home the provisions, with light hearts. As for Billy his ears burned by the time Frank got through reading him a lecture.

"I'm sorry," he said bravely, "and I won't do it again. Gee! talk about 'press the button and we'll do the rest.'"

"They nearly did it - didn't they," laughed Frank, his good humor quite restored.

CHAPTIER VII

A TRAITOR IN CAMP

It was a week later, and the launch having towed the expedition as far up the river as Frank decided was necessary - before they struck out into the unknown land of the cannibals, winged men, and the ivory hoard - had returned to civilization several days before, carrying with it letters from all the adventurers which they felt might be the last they would write for some time. The spot selected for the permanent camp was a sort of park-like space covered at its edges with masses of manioc and banana bushes. Beyond towered huge tropical trees and beyond these again the blue outlines of the distant Moon Mountains in which, according to old Barr's map, lay the ivory cache.

It had been a busy week. The Golden Eagle II had been re-erected and her own wireless and the field wireless apparatus put in order. As our readers who have followed this series are familiar with the manner of setting up the great Chester aeroplane and her fittings, it would be tedious to repeat the description of the process. Suffice it to say that thanks to the clever simplicity of the "knock-down" arrangement, by which the ship could be taken apart and set up again, the operation of equipping her for active work was a comparatively light one. The extra gasoline and supplies for the camp in general were stored in a separate tent removed from the circle in which the boys' tents and those of Ben Stubbs and Professor Wiseman were pitched.

There was, too, a newcomer in the camp - a Portuguese named Diego de Barros. He was not a particularly well-favored individual, but he bore the reputation of having great power over the natives and of being very friendly to the white traders who penetrated into the interior. Once or twice there had been ugly talk about his being in league with the Arab slave and ivory traders, but he had managed to clear his name and along the Ivory Coast enjoyed the reputation of being an honest, reliable man. He had joined the boys' camp a few days before and his manner of coming was this.

While everybody was busy getting things in shape there had come a loud hail from the quarters of the native helpers, just outside the white man's encampment, announcing that a canoe was coming up the river. All hands had hastened to the river bank to find de Barros just putting his foot ashore from the canoe in which two natives had paddled him from the coast. He had with him some bales of cotton goods and a few gewgaws of various kinds and was bound, so he said, on a trading expedition into the back country. Further down the river he had heard, he explained, that the boys were camped where he found them, and he had determined to pay them a visit. The brief stay that the boys had interpreted this as meaning, however, had extended itself into three days and still Diego showed no inclination to leave.

"If he doesn't move on soon I shall be compelled to ask him to go," said Frank in an annoyed tone to Harry. "I don't want to be inhospitable, but we can't afford to have strangers hanging round the camp, there is too much at stake."

Harry agreed with him and the two boys decided to tell the Portuguese that evening as tactfully as possible that they were on a private enterprise and could not accommodate strangers. This decision arrived at, Frank turned to the steel strong box that was never out of his sight and drew from it the precious map of the Moon Mountains. Seated at the little camp-table - (the conversation just related had taken place in the Boy Aviators' tent) - the two pored over the document for hours. With dividers, compass and parallel rulers Frank, who was a skilled navigator, laid out an aerial course that would bring them, he calculated, unerringly to the spot marked by a red cross where - so old Luther Barr declared - lay the ivory that was to save Mr. Beasley from financial ruin and disgrace.

Frank laid his finger on the spot and exclaimed enthusiastically:

"There it is, Harry, and we are not so far from it now. In a few days we shall know whether we are on a wild-goose chase or not."

"Why, no doubt has ever entered your head that the ivory is there?" questioned Harry.

"Well, old fellow, you know there are others interested in this ivory beside ourselves - Muley-Hassan for instance."

"You think he had got ahead of us?"

"I did not say I thought so, I only say that it is possible that he may have done so."

"How could he have got wind of our coming?"

"In Africa there is a sort of underground wire for news," replied Frank. "I have no doubt that hundreds of natives far in the interior are by this time apprised of our coming."

Harry looked alarmed.

"That's bad," he said.

"Well, it couldn't be helped: but we may have other enemies nearer at hand."

"What do you mean?"

"That I don't like the looks of that Portuguese fellow. If he got wind of what we are doing he would be likely to ruin the whole object of our expedition."

"That's so. We'll have to get rid of him."

"Well, we are going to, and if he won't go for gentle means we'll try rough ones."

"Hullo, what's that?" exclaimed Harry suddenly.

The flap at the end of the tent toward which both of their backs had been turned had been suddenly drawn aside and in one quick, backward glance Harry made out the smiling figure of de Barros standing in the doorway. It might have been fancy, but he thought for a minute that the Portuguese had a peculiarly villainous expression on his dark, handsome features.

"Ah, senors," he said, as Frank, with a quick movement swept the map off the table - but not before de Barros's quick eyes had spied it. Fearing to replace the precious chart in the strong box, while the Portuguese lingered, Frank tucked it into his pocket.

"Ah, senors, good afternoon," grinned the unwelcome visitor. "I have come to say 'adios.' I am going up the river to-night and may not see you again for a long time."

"I am sorry to have you leave," said Frank with a heartfelt wish that de Barros would hasten his departure.

"I knew you would be," smiled the Portuguese, "but it is the lot of man to meet and part. Adios, senors, I go to make ready."

He vanished as suddenly as he had come upon the scene.

"What do you make of that?" inquired Harry.

"I don't know what to think. I have an idea that he was listening to every word of our conversation just now and that he saw the map before I had time to sweep it off the table."

Harry looked vexed.

"That's tough luck," he said. "If he overheard even a part of our talk he must realize the object of our presence in Africa. And," he went on, "I don't know a man on the Dark Continent whom I would trust less than Diego de Barros, even the little we've seen of him."

"It can't be helped now," said Frank briefly; "come on, let's go and put the finishing touches on the good old Eagle."

They worked the rest of the afternoon putting the big aeroplane in shape for her flight to the Moon Mountains which it had been determined to make the next day. It was almost dusk when Harry, who was working over the engines, asked Frank for the reserve park-plug box.

"It's in one of the canoes. I'll go and get it," said Frank, and at once set off toward the river bank for that purpose. His path led through a thick grove of bamboos which hid him from the view of the camp after he had traversed a short distance. As he merged on the river bank, whistling softly to himself, the young leader suddenly felt himself pinioned by arms that seemed of enormous strength - though, as the attack had come from behind, he could not see the faces of his assailants. The next minute he was lying flat on his back, bound and helpless with a bit of greasy cloth shoved in his mouth for a gag.

"Keep still, senor, and you shall not be hurt;" said a quiet voice near at hand, and Frank saw bending above him the sallow features of the smiling Portuguese.

"I just have to trouble you for that map I saw you put in your pocket, that is all," went on his captor, while the two huge negroes who had made Frank prisoner stood to one side immovable as carved figures,

"It is lucky for me that you came down to the river bank," grinned the Portuguese as he ran his hand over Frank's clothes, to ascertain the hiding-place of the precious map of the ivory cache, "otherwise I should have had to delay my departure till to-night, and possibly have cut your throat while you slept."

Frank felt as if his heart would burst with rage and mortification as the greasy, smiling Portuguese deliberately drew out the priceless document and gazed at it in triumph. He laid it on the ground beside him while lie resumed his search for other clues.

"That ivory belongs to my master - Muley-Hassan - now," he sneered; "did you think for a minute that we would ever let you white fools get it back again."

It was well for the Portuguese that Frank's hands were not free then. Had they been the dark-skinned traitor would have had a fight on his hands in a few seconds. But suddenly events took a strange turn.

The two blacks uttered a sharp cry of warning as the bushes parted and a huge form dashed out, whirling about its head a glistening axe.

It was Sikaso!

The next minute would have been Diego's last but that his two followers lifted him to his feet and, picking him up like a child, ran for his canoe with him. With a few rapid strokes they were in midstream and paddling up the river with powerful strokes while Sikaso raged impotently on the shore.

"Oh for one of the white men's fire-tubes!" he sighed,

and even as he spoke a sharp reminder of the efficiency of these same "fire-tubes" whizzed past his ear in the shape of a bullet from Diego's revolver.

In a few steps the old black was beside his young leader and with a couple of strokes of his keen blade had set him free.

"Quick, Sikaso; the canoes - we must pursue him. Call the boys and Ben while I cast off the canoes. Quick, we have not a minute to lose."

Although Diego in his hurry had not carried off the map but left it lying on the ground, still Frank realized that the Portuguese had not actually needed the document to aid Muley-Hassan to find the cache. The Arab was no doubt familiar with the location anyway, but to head off all danger of the boys getting there first, it was vital to stop Diego at all costs. In a few bounds Frank reached the little indentation in the bank where the canoes were kept.

As he gained it he fell back with a groan and, brave boy as he was, he leaned weakly against a tree for support as the true extent of the crushing disaster that had occurred was borne in on him.

The canoes were gone!

The cunning rascal, Diego, had devised his plan well.

The painters of all the craft had been cut, and by this time they were doubtless miles down the stream.

CHAPTER VIII

A BATTLE IN THE AIR

The consternation with which the news of the loss of the canoes was received by the young adventurers may be imagined. It meant that they were cut off from communication with the coast entirely unless some unforeseen circumstances arose. But in spite of the oppression that naturally affected them at the first news of their serious loss, Frank's confident manner had its effect in restoring some sort of hope. Like the born leader that he was, Frank, the minute he recovered from the first effects of his bitter dismay, set about cheering up the others.

"We've always got the Golden Eagle," he comforted, "and anyway it's likely if no one stops them, that some at least of the canoes will drift down the river to the coast. M. Desplaines will no doubt be able to surmise something serious has happened when he hears of their arrival and will send aid. In the meantime we have to consider what we are to do about the ivory cache."

As a matter of fact, as the boys learned later, none of the canoes ever reached the coast, being intercepted by river-tribes.

"I vote for going ahead," cried Harry, catching the

optimistic note that his brother's words conveyed.

"That's the stuff," cried the young leader, "that is exactly what I was going to propose."

"How about you, red-top?" asked Billy turning to Lathrop.

"Of course I'm on," was the reply.

"I hate to dash your enthusiasm," said Frank, "but you fellows must see that it is impossible for all of us to go. My plan is to take Ben Stubbs along and leave you fellows and Sikaso here to guard the camp. Then, too, there is the possibility of a relief expedition arriving as soon as they discover that we have lost our canoes."

Old Sikaso leant apart on his mighty war-axe. He seemed to regret heartily that he had not had an opportunity of testing its metal on the head of the knavish Portuguese.

"What do you say to that plan, Sikaso?" asked Frank, who already placed a high value on the old warrior's judgment.

"That it is good, my white brother. Sikaso will stay with the four-eyed one and the ruddy-haired one and we will see that no harm comes to the camp of the young white warriors."

"It is well," replied Frank, who was falling into a trick of addressing the stately Krooman in the same grandiloquent fashion as the latter was in the habit of using, "I place my trust in you."

"Hum," snorted Billy, "four-eyes and red-top that's a nice combination for you! I'd like to do something to show that old chap that we can do just as much as anyone else when it comes to a show-down."

This remark, however, was made sotto voce to Lathrop, as Billy really stood in great awe of the six foot-two of ebony flesh and muscle that was Sikaso.

But Stubbs was delighted at his selection to accompany the boys in their aerial dash for the ivory cache. He spent half the night by lantern light pottering about the great craft and stocking her up with provisions and equipment for the journey. By the time he had finished it was almost midnight and he turned in to join the boys in the land of dreams where Frank and Harry, and doubtless the others, too, were already busy shooting down Diegos and hippopotami and flitting through the air above the great African forest and performing all sorts of wonderful feats.

At dawn everybody was up and about and after farewells had been said the Chester boys and their sturdy old companion clambered into the chassis of their craft. Frank had already laid out his course, which lay about two points west of north. The boy calculated that this direction would bring them within a few miles at any rate of the cache. To find it they would have to trust to persistence and a modicum of luck.

Old Sikaso, who had, of course, never seen anything even remotely resembling an aeroplane, stood apart from the excited group clustered about the big craft and gazed at it with astonishment, not unmixed with awe. The other Kroomen - the packers and camp-workers, however, gathered close about the machine and the boys had a lot of trouble keeping their busy fingers from unscrewing nuts and loosening turnbuckles.

"Anything more like a pack of monkeys on a picnic I never saw," exclaimed Billy as for the twentieth time he chased a long, skinny native away from the propellers, where he would have assuredly been decapitated if he had remained till the engine was started.

A few turns with the clutch thrown out showed the engine was running as true as on the day the Golden Eagle made her trial trip. The muffler was cut out and the effect of the wide-open exhaust on the Kroomen was magical. Within a second from the time that Harry threw in the switch and the gatling gun uproar of the exhaust made itself manifest, not a solitary one was to be seen. From the greenery of the jungle that rimmed the clearing, however, their frightened faces could be seen peering, like some strange sort of fruit among the tropical growth. Only old Sikaso stood his ground.

But even that stolid old warrior grasped his great war-axe a little tighter and stood erect as if about to face an unknown enemy as jets of blue flame and smoke shot from the detonating exhaust.

"All ready, Harry?" cried Frank to the younger boy who was at his old station by the engines.

"Ay, ay!" came the response in a hearty tone. "Then let her go."

With a quick movement Frank threw in the clutch.

The mighty propellers began to beat the air with the whirring sound of a swarm of gigantic locusts in full flight, and after a short run the great aeroplane took the air in a long graceful rising arc. Half an hour later, to the watchers in the camp, she was little more than a speck against the sky.

Frank, his eye constantly on the compass, kept the ship on a true course for the Moon Mountains which, now that they were flying far above the dense forest region, lay a rugged mass of blue and brown, piled like some giant's playthings - on the northwestern horizon.

Even from the distance at which the boys viewed them they conveyed an almost sinister impression in their rugged shapes. Their harsh outlines cut the sky in a serrated line like the teeth of a huge saw.

"Look, look, Frank!" shouted Harry suddenly as they were passing high over a small clearing.

Both Frank and Ben peered over the side in answer to the boy's excited hail.

Far below them was a strange sight.

In the center of the clearing were four huge African elephants solemnly conducting a sort of Brobding-naggian game of tag. One of the great beasts would tap the other with its trunk and then would scamper away till it in turn was "tapped" by a blow that would have swept a small regiment off its feet.

Frank pushed over a lever and swung the ship in a circle so that they might watch the great animals to better advantage. Suddenly the boys saw one of the elephants, evidently seized by sudden rage, start goring one of its companions with its huge tusks. The attacked animal had no chance, and but for the boys would speedily have been killed.

"I'm going to give that big bully a shot," exclaimed Harry, and he got out one of the heavy rifles from the rack under the starboard transom.

"Wait, I'll drop a bit," said Frank.

In response to his manipulation the aeroplane dropped till she hovered not more than two hundred feet above the great animals. Then a strange thing happened. The shadow of the craft fell upon the center of the clearing in front of the dueling beasts and the on-looking pachyderms, and as it did so the bully stopped goring its mate and gave a snort of astonishment.

Its note of surprise quickly changed to a loud trumpet of terror as the great pachyderm saw swooping above it what must have appeared to it an aerial inhabitant even larger than itself. Its note of fright was echoed in a chorus that sounded like an assemblage of cracked trumpets as the others also sensed the impending danger.

"Now let him have it," shouted Frank.

Harry's rifle cracked and the big bully staggered. Twice more the boy fired and the huge creature staggered on to its knees and then with a mighty groan rolled over on its side. The others, even the wounded one, had made off as soon as they had caught sight of the hovering Golden Eagle.

Even from the height at which they were the boys could see that the dead animal had an enormous pair of tusks, no doubt extremely valuable.

"We ought to have them there figure-heads," commented Ben Stubbs. "What do you say if we drop down and get them?"

Frank looked at his watch. It was half-past nine.

"We cannot be more than a hundred miles now from the foot of the range," he said, "and I suppose we have plenty of time. We might as well drop and get them as let some native tribe have the find and then get skinned out of them by an Arab trader."

As he spoke the boy set the planes for descending and the Golden Eagle settled down - after a few minutes rapid falling - fairly in the center of the clearing. It was almost a fairylike spot. On every side it was hedged in by the densest jungle vegetation, the solid walls being broken here and there by elephant paths leading off into the green tangle.

The little glade in which the Golden Eagle had settled was covered with short, yellow grass and had been trampled almost bare of vegetation, apparently by the gambols of countless generations of elephants.

"This must be one of the elephant playgrounds I have read about," exclaimed Harry, looking about him.

"No doubt it is," replied Frank. "But look at those tusks, why there's ivory enough there alone to give us all a nice wad of pocket money."

Ben Stubbs, with one of the small axes, at once set about hacking out the dead elephant's huge tusks and a long job it was. Finally, however, he managed to cut them free and clear and the boys loaded them into the aeroplane.

"Now we are all ready for a fresh start," said Frank as they clambered in after him and settled down in their places; but a startling interruption occurred.

With a wild yell, that struck a sudden chill to the heart of every one of the little group, a band of beings that at first sight looked like nothing so much as huge gorillas, burst from the forest on every side.

Their heads were misshapen and flat and their protruding lips were daubed with white and red clay which gave them a ghastly unearthly look. From their ears hung huge ivory pendants. They carried elephant skin shields and were armed with spears and bow and arrows. As if they did not consider themselves sufficiently hideous, several of the tribe had cut their faces in long stripes and the hardly healed scars of these wounds rendered their already sinister faces terrifying indeed.

Desperately Harry threw over the wheel and the engines started faithfully to respond but not before half a dozen of the savages had thrown themselves on to the aeroplane.

Their weight held her down although she scudded over the ground; and in the meantime the other natives started pouring a shower of arrows and spears into her. Fortunately none of these struck the boys although Frank felt an arrow whiz through the loose sleeve of his shirt.

"Get those fellows off or I can't get the ship up," he yelled.

Harry and Ben Stubbs fired their automatics into the clinging mass of savages.

Two dropped and the aeroplane began to rise but the others desperately clung on.

"Get 'em off," shouted Frank, as he desperately strove to raise the air-craft.

As he spoke he fell back with a cry of pain.

An arrow had struck him on the shoulder inflicting a painful wound.

Like a flash Harry took in the situation and leaped to the steering wheel. As he did so the savage with whom he had been contending clambered clear into the chassis. At the same instant Ben Stubbs' revolver dispatched the last of the men clinging to the planes and the Golden Eagle began to rise.

As she shot upward the savage who had climbed into the chassis gave a wild shriek of real terror. But his outburst didn't come before he had made a savage lunge at Ben Stubbs with a short heavy knife. The solo adventurer dived under the black's arm and struck it upward as he lunged and the weapon went whirling groundward out of the air-ship.

With a cry of despair the savage rushed to the edge of the car and was about to throw himself into empty air when Ben leaped forward to try to restrain him.

But it was too late.

As the boys' sturdy companion gallantly attempted to save the savage's life a flight of arrows whizzed up from below.

With a groan the man on the edge of the car pitched forward into open space, pierced to the heart with an arrow sped by one of his own tribesmen. Down he shot like a stone to the earth below, while the Golden Eagle - as if rejoicing in her escape, shot upward and onward.

CHAPTER IX

THE VOICE OF THE MOUNTAIN

Frank's wound fortunately turned out to be nothing very serious - though painful enough - and after it had been treated with antiseptics from the medicine chest he declared that, aside from the stiffness and soreness, he felt no ill effect.

"Those fellows certainly gave us a sample of what we may expect," remarked Harry, examining the hole in his shirt where the arrow had ripped through.

"It was quite as narrow an escape as I care to experience," agreed Frank. "How about you, Ben?"

"Wall," said the old adventurer, "I don't know as how I think that kind of excitement is as beneficial fer the health as the rest cure."

Meanwhile the Golden Eagle, plowing through the clear African air at fifty miles an hour, rapidly drew nearer and nearer to the mysterious Moon Mountains.

As they neared the range the extraordinary character of it was revealed more and more clearly. Seamed with deep gloomy abysses and almost bare of vegetation, except a few scanty groves of palms and the hardier tropical trees, they seemed indeed fitted to be the theater of dark mysteries and the haunt of savage tribes.

"Well," exclaimed Harry, as be scrutinized the strange mountain mass through the glasses, "I should say that if those Winged Men are to be found anywhere, here is where they'd reside."

"I should think they'd use their wings to get out - a nastier looking lot of mountains I never saw," was Ben's reply.

Frank made no comment, but the sinister character of the mountains they were so rapidly approaching impressed itself on his mind nevertheless. Eagerly he scanned the range for the first sign of "The Upturned Face." Harry and Ben, too, gave quite as eager scrutiny toward the discovery of this striking mark of the ivory's hiding-place.

All at once it shot into view with a suddenness that made the boys' beads swim.

It was as clear as daylight. The line of the mountain for which Frank had the Golden Eagle II now directly headed was unmistakably the outline also of a hawk-nosed facet.

If the mountains themselves had an evil, menacing look, the stone face possessed this same quality in an infinitely greater degree.

"Well, if we've got to go looking for ivory right under that face the sooner we find it the better," exclaimed Ben. "I'd hate to be shipmates with the fellow who sat for that portrait."

"No human being ever sat for it, Ben," laughed Frank; "it's a mere freak of nature which has so disposed the mountain mass at this point as to give the semblance of what the map-maker terms The Upturned Face."

"Well, if I had a mug like that I'd turn it down instead of up before some one did it for me," was Ben's comment.

The Golden Eagle landed on a plateau about halfway up the mountain, beneath the upturned face. It made an almost ideal camping-place, considering the rugged nature of their surroundings. In one part of it a small grove of bananas and palms had taken root, and their smiling greenery offered a refreshing contrast to the dark oppressive gloom of the giant rock masses piled all about. From the center of this oasis in the rocky range bubbled a tiny spring of water as clear and cold as if it had been filtered and iced. Frank's first act was to send out a wireless to the River Camp, telling of their arrival.

"Well, thank goodness, we've got something green and pleasant to look at," remarked Ben, as they set about transforming the chassis of the Golden Eagle into a comfortable tent by means of running up the canvas curtains on the aluminum frames provided for that purpose. Thus equipped, the chassis served the uses of an improved tent, as the floor was well above the ground and out of all danger of the unwholesome, vapors rising from the ground and also the scorpions and other reptiles.

But if the oasis itself was a pretty spot, it was made

doubly so by the contrast it afforded to the scenery surrounding it. On all sides shot up frowning walls of rugged black rock which seemed to have been torn and ripped in some remote period by a terrific convulsion of nature. In places, too, the rock masses seemed to have been seared by subterranean fires. Frank gazed upward at the terrific character of the scenery about them.

"We shall need the rope-ladder," he announced suddenly after a long silence.

"The rope-ladder?" inquired Harry, "what for?"

Frank laughed.

"I mean the rope-ladder we use in the Golden Eagle. As you know, the only way to locate the cache is to strike a direct line down from the nose of the upturned face. That will bring us to the small cairn or pile of rocks that marks the Arab's hiding-place."

"He could hardly have chosen a better," remarked Harry. "Who would ever guess, unless they had the key to the mystery, that these mountains held such a fortune in tusks."

The rest of that day was spent in overhauling the outfit which they would need to use on their expedition of the morrow. Luckily the boots they wore had been fitted with "hob-nails" so that they were ideal for the tough climb that they had ahead of them. Each member of the three was to carry a pick and of course they all were to be armed, carrying several rounds of ammunition each in their cartridge-belts.

That night after a supper of fried ham, canned corn and pancakes - all cooked by the skilful Ben over a fire of wood collected from the little grove - Frank sent out a wireless to the members of the camp on the river bank and felt much reassured when Lathrop's "All well - good luck," came back through the air. It was delightfully cool on the mountain-side after the oppressive fetid air of the river and its neighborhood, and as Ben had remarked before they turned in:

"Fine weather for sleeping."

But sleep would not come to Frank. He tossed and turned on his transom bed and several times gazed out into the night through the canvas curtains. An unaccountable feeling of unrest possessed him. Could they get the ivory out of the cache before Muley-Hassan and his band arrived by land?

Fast as they had traveled through the air Frank realized that the Arab, who doubtless by this time had been informed by the treacherous Diego of the boys' bold dash, would push on at furious speed in order to head them off. That he would come accompanied by a well-armed band Frank could not doubt. He and Harry and Ben could only put up a feeble resistance against such an attack. There was only one chance to secure the ivory and that was to get at it before the Arab arrived. It all depended then on how quickly they could find the cache. Frank lit the lantern and shielding it so that it would not strike in the eyes of his sleeping brother, drew out the map and scanned it attentively.

Yes, here were the directions written in the queer hand of Muley-Hassan's follower.

"A line from the nose straight down to the cairn of stones."

It seemed simple enough and certainly the nose of the Upturned Face was as clearly to be made out as a ship at sea. But Frank had been too long trained in the hard school of adventure to underestimate the difficulties of any piece of work. They faced a hard job and none realized the fact better than the young leader.

At last he blew the lantern out and once more composed himself to sleep. He was just dozing off when a sufficiently startling interruption occurred. One which drove all further thoughts of rest from his head.

It was an extraordinary sound that brought the boy out of his bed with a bound and caused him to clutch his revolver with a heart that beat loud and thick in spite of himself.

Clutching his weapon the boy rushed to the door of the chassis tent and gazed out.

There was a bright moon which threw into inky blackness the depressions of the rugged mountains and threw up their projections into a blue glare. It was almost as light as day under that wonderful African moon. Had there been any one near the boy must have been able to see them.

But look as he would there was not a soul in sight. All about him stretched the barren frowning mountains sleeping under the moon.

But the sound that he had heard?

There was no mistaking it. It had been too like the low humming of a human voice for him to have been misled. Perhaps he had been dreaming?

But as if to give the lie to any such supposition the strange sound that had so alarmed him at that moment made itself manifest once more:

"A-hooo-A-AH-HOOO-00-a-ho-ho-ho-o-!"

It started softly and gradually ran up the scale till it reached a crescendo shout and then died out in a soft sound like a woman's wail. Heard anywhere the sound would have been alarming enough, but coming as it did in the midst of these unknown, mysterious Mountains of the Moon it struck a chill to the boy's heart and caused his scalp to tighten in a manner that even the bravest man or boy in the world would have had no reason to feel shame over.

A human enemy, a foe he could see, Frank would have faced with iron nerve; but this strange wailing noise coming from what quarter of the compass he could not judge - was so uncanny that he was really disturbed. He bounded into the chassis and roused Ben and Harry. He had hardly whispered to them the extraordinary intelligence when again the voice arose.

"A-ho-ho-h-o-o-o-A-h-hoo-ho-AH-HO-HO-O-O-O-AH-ho-h-o-o-o-o-o-o!"

"Well, who?" roared Ben angrily, "come out and show yourself, you human hyena, and I'll put so much lead in your system you'll be worth a nickel a pound. Come, you old Ah-Hoo, and I'll show you who I am quick enough - shiver my topsails!"

But the only reply to Ben's tirade was the dismal echo of his voice among the rocky chasms.

"Shiver my topsails!" roared the echo and then the hills bandied the cry about from ridge to ridge till it died out in a whisper:

"My topsails!"

"Hum," remarked Ben, "I don't think I'll talk so loud around here. There seem to be a lot of folks listening. Such a dreary hole as this I never - "

"Never," sighed the echoes, " - never."

"Here, I can't stand this," cried Harry. "I'm going to send a bullet up there the next time that fellow starts 'Ah-hooing.'"

But as the strange mournful cry rang out once more the boys paused in bewilderment.

There was no locating the sound.

It seemed to fill the air. To come from every quarter of the compass at once.

CHAPTER X

THE ARAB'S CACHE

The mysterious cries were not repeated that night although the boys laid awake till daylight listening for any repetition. No theory they could advance, although these ranged all the way from cannibals and gorillas to ghosts, had any effect on the solution of the mystery. They finally agreed to trust to solving it in some chance way, and like sensible boys did not continue to worry themselves over the unsolvable.

Frank's first action was to send out a wireless to the river camp and to his great relief he found that events there were still proceeding with the same regularity as before. Nothing had occurred to mar the even life of the young adventurers left behind. This was the tenor of the message, but there was something about it that worried Frank. Lathrop, he knew, was an expert wireless operator, but the sending that he performed that morning was so jerky and irregular that the rankest amateur might have done better.

"What is the matter?" asked Frank sharply after the sending had become even more unskilled and shaky.

There was no answer; which caused Frank a vague feeling of apprehension. He speedily drove this impression from his mind, however, with:

"Pshaw! the sleepless night I passed has made me nervous."

After breakfast there was so much to be done that there was no more time to waste on gloomy forebodings and the boys started, as soon as the camp had been put in order, on their expedition up the mountain-side to the Upturned Face - which was to be the starting point for the uncovering of the secret ivory hoard.

The climb was quite as stiff as Frank had anticipated and, laden as they were with the rope-ladder and the other equipment, it was rendered even tougher. All three carried water-canteens covered with wet felt, containing half-a-gallon each. Frank had insisted on this as it was doubtful if they could find water at the summit of the mountain.

As the sun rose higher in the sky and beat down on the bare rock ridges over which the adventurers were making their way, it became as uncomfortable as any expedition on which the boys had ever beer engaged.

"Talk about New Mexico or Death Valley," exclaimed Harry, "I feel like a piece of butter rolled up in a paper and I've melted."

"I feel like a Welsh rarebit myself," laughed Frank, "how about you, Ben?"

"I feel like a pot of boiling tar with a fire lighted under me," growled the veteran angrily; "consarn these rocks, I'd give a whole lot for a bit of that shade we left behind us."

Despite the discomfort and the heat, however, they struggled on up the mountain-side, frequently using the rope-ladder to get over rough places, and at about noon they stood beneath the steep rock cliff that formed the nose of the upturned face.

It was easy enough then to reach a spot below the tip and Frank, with a long cord he had brought for the purpose, laid out a straight line from the point down the southern slope of the mountain-side. While they were busy about this they were startled by a repetition of the same strange cry, half-warning, half-savage, that they had been so alarmed by the night before.

"A-ho-o-o-o-AH-H-O-O-O-a-h-o-o-hoo-o-o-o-o!"

"Great Scott," yelled Harry, "what on earth do you think of that?"

Frank - considerably startled himself - had, however, made a determined effort to ascertain the source of the sound as it rose and fell in its strange cadence.

"I've got it!" he shouted; now with a cry of triumph.

"Got what?" cried Harry, as if he feared his brother had suddenly become infected with some strange complaint - "rabies or the pip?"

"The noise - I mean I know where it comes from," cried the excited boy.

"Where?" chorused Ben and Harry.

"From somewhere about the Upturned Face," cried Frank triumphantly, "Hark!"

The strange wailing cry rang out once more. They all listened intently.

Sure enough it seemed to proceed from the sinister countenance carved in the living rock above them.

"Well, here's where we end this mystery for all time," shouted Frank, drawing his revolver, "who is game to follow me?"

Of course Harry and Ben rushed to his side, and while the echo of the mysterious cry was still sobbing and sighing among the crags they dashed back up the mountain-side utterly oblivious now to the heat or anything but their determination to discover who or what had uttered the extraordinary cry. The side of the nose - or the nostril so to speak - was formed of a wall of rock fully twelve feet in height.

"You fellows give me a boost up there and I'll travel right along the face till I find out where the racket comes from."

On Ben's strong shoulders Frank was soon hoisted up to a height where he could lay hold of a projecting bit of rock and shin himself up on to the top of the nose.

"Look out he doesn't think you are a fly and try to brush you off," laughed Harry from below.

"No danger of that," shouted back Frank, "unless I lit on him in the Golden Eagle."

The surface of the face was as remarkable as its profile.

Apparently some forgotten tribe had at some time or other been struck by the facial outline of the rocks and had cut into the flat surface, which was upturned to the sky, eyes and a mouth, the latter well provided with teeth, in each of which was drilled a tiny triangular hole.

While Frank was puzzling over the meaning of these apertures there came a repetition of the weird cry, but this time the lad was so startled that he almost lost his balance and fell backward.

The call seemed to proceed from his very feet. Then, all at once, he realized what it was.

The strange sounds proceeded from the mouth of the stone face.

Frank ran to the edge of the steep declivity that formed the nose.

"Say, Harry, and you too, Ben, examine the surface below there very carefully for any holes. They will probably be small ones and in a row."

"None this side," announced the searchers after a lengthy quest.

"Try the other," ordered Frank.

They did so and after a few minutes of careful scrutiny Harry shouted that they had found a row of small holes pierced in the rock just below where Frank stood.

"Then we have solved the mystery of the voice," exclaimed Frank.

"What do you mean?" demanded Harry.

"That it is nothing more or less than an arrangement of holes through which, when the wind blows in a stiff puff, air is forced with violence enough to cause the cry that disturbed us so much last night," was the reply.

This indeed was the solution, and had the boys known it there are many such rocks in Africa, carved out by some forgotten race, and the weird cries that the vent-holes give out in the wind doubtless acted as a powerful "fetish" to keep away troublesome enemies.

"No wonder the niggers down below don't come near the Moon Mountains," said Harry, as they all buckled over the simple explanation of the phenomenon that had caused them so much alarm. "I wouldn't care to, myself, unless I knew just what made that cry."

"It certainly was as depressing as anything I ever heard," said Frank, "and now having solved the great mystery - let's get back to work."

The three adventurers went at the job with a will. The line was about a hundred feet long and the method of procedure was this: Frank tested the straightness of the line, as accurately as possible with his eye, while Ben and Harry carried it stretched between them. The end of each hundred feet was signalized by a stone, and Harry, who was at the end of the line, carried his end to this mark before they laid out a fresh hundred feet. In this way they must have measured off very nearly half-a-mile of the mountain-side when Frank gave a sudden sharp cry and pointed to a depression in the dark range immediately below them. As the others looked they echoed his cry and gave a dash forward.

Directly beneath them, about in the center of the little dip, was a cairn of rough stones perhaps four feet in height. In a few bounds they had reached the pile, which they knew meant the discovery of the ivory cache and the end of the most difficult part of their expedition. Little did they imagine the amazing things that were yet to happen to them and of which they were but on the threshold.

"Good Lord, look at that, boys!" exclaimed Frank, as they stood at the foot of the cairn.

There was a good reason for the boy's exclamation.

Distributed around the base of the pile were a dozen or, more human skulls.

"Are they those of white men?" asked Harry in an awed tone. Frank shook his head.

"No, they are those of negroes I believe," he replied after a careful examination, "and I imagine that Muley-Hassan killed them after they erected the cache so that they would not be able to spread the knowledge of its whereabouts to any of the marauding tribes who might even brave the ghostly voice when such a great treasure of ivory tempted."

A shout from Ben, who had been walking round the pile examining it from every view-point interrupted them. They looked up and saw the old adventurer pointing to the mountain summit where it cut the sky. Outlined against the deep azure was the object that had caused his exclamation. It was the figure of a man that had apparently been watching them intently.

But as they gazed the strange, crouched form suddenly vanished.

CHAPTER XI

THE AGE OF SIKASO

It was late afternoon of the day that Frank, Harry and Ben had left the River Camp. Lathrop, Billy, Barnes and old Sikaso had wandered into the jungle with their rifles, intent on bringing down some sort of game to replenish the camp larder. For hours they tramped about in the thick jungle and a fair measure of success had fallen to their rifles. Shortly before sundown the trio met in a glade not more than a mile from the camp and compared notes. To Billy's gun had fallen a plump young deer and Lathrop had brought down, not without a feeling of considerable pride, a species of wild hog which Sikaso proclaimed with a grunt was "heap good."

Flushed with triumph and carrying their own bag, the young hunters set out for the camp, arriving there at dusk. As has been told, it was not long after that that Frank's wireless from the Moon Mountains winged its way through the air and Lathrop was able to flash back in response an "all-well" message. The boys turned in early, Billy and Lathrop to their tent and old Sikaso to the rough shelter he had contrived for himself and which he declared was far more comfortable than any tent. Like a wild beast the savage old warrior disliked to have anything approaching a roof over him. It appeared to savor too much of a trap of some kind.

Billy might have been asleep five hours or so and it was approaching midnight when he heard a noise outside the tent door and a second later old Sikaso announced his presence by a whispered:

"Awake, Four-eyes, there is danger."

"What do you mean, Sikaso," demanded the half asleep reporter, "danger to our friends?"

"No; to us, and here and soon," was the disquieting response, "arouse your friend. We have no time to lose."

Billy was wide awake now and made a motion as if he would light the lantern.

Sikaso stopped him with a quick gesture.

"Do not light the lamp, my white brother," he whispered in the same tense tones, "to do so would be to reveal to those who are now approaching that we are awake and expect them. Rather let us pretend that we are unaware that they come and spring upon them like the leopard when she is least expected."

"Yes, but - " exclaimed Billy in a bewildered tone, "what do you mean, Sikaso, what enemies are coming? How do you know that they are approaching?"

"I have seen it in the smoke," was the somber reply; "the smoke never lies. After I lay down on my skins I could not sleep, I felt there was danger approaching us.

From where I knew not. So I made the "fetish" fire. In it I saw a band of men coming toward us down the river and at the head of them was a dark man - a man you know well, my white brother with the four eyes."

"Diego!" exclaimed Billy divining the other's thought.

"Yes, Diego; cursed be the day that my war-axe did not cleave his ugly skull; but beside Diego there is another. Hearken to the words of Sikaso, the elephant in his rage is not more merciless, the serpent not more cunning, the crocodile not more savage in onslaught than this other. He is Muley-Hassan, the Arab, and the deeds he has done, my brother, when recounted turn strong men's blood to water."

Small wonder that Billy, as he hastily roused Lathrop, felt a shudder run through him. He had heard enough from Frank of the ways of Muley-Hassan to know that they could not well fall into the hands of a more pitiless foe and that now, with the Golden Eagle gone and the Boy Aviators already at the ivory cache, it was probable that the slave-dealer's rage would render him even more savage than was his wont.

In a few rapidly whispered words Billy apprised Lathrop of the situation. Like Billy, the other boy had no lack of pluck but his heart sank, as had his companion's, as he sensed the full meaning of Sikaso's warning.

"But perhaps the smoke was mistaken," he said eagerly, willing to grasp even at that straw of hope; but the old warrior's answer dashed his aspirations to the ground.

"The smoke is never mistaken," he said simply; but with such calm conviction that the boys, despite themselves, realized that the old Krooman had really the knowledge of grave peril approaching.

"Had we not better arm the other Kroomen?" asked Billy anxiously.

"It would be useless," was Sikaso's reply, "they are cowards. At the first sight of blood they would run to the forest like the sons of weaklings that they are."

"We must rouse Professor Wiseman at once," cried Billy.

"It is well," muttered Sikaso, "we shall need every man who can hold a rifle to-night but the professor is old, my brothers, and his heart is as a woman's."

"Well, he'll have to fight," said Billy with bloodthirsty determination. "I for one am not going to stand calmly by and have my throat cut, or worse still be taken prisoner by this old Muley-Hassan."

Old Sikaso glanced approvingly at him.

"Well spoken, Four-eyes," said he; "spoken like a son of a warrior."

Billy's ears tingled at the compliment, which was really in the old African's opinion the highest that could be paid to a man or a boy, and hurried off to wake "the bugologist" as be disrespectfully termed the professor. To his surprise, for he more than half expected an outbreak, Professor Wiseman did not appear particularly concerned at the news that Diego, and Muley-Hassan were - as the boys had every reason to believe - at that moment advancing on the camp.

"I will dress myself with all alacrity," he said, "and join you in your tent, but I must say I don't believe in all this witchcraft."

"Will this Muley-Hassan be well armed?" asked Billy, in a voice which was rather shaky, of their black friend.

"Plenty rifles," was Sikaso's brief reply.

"Don't you want a rifle or at least a heavy caliber shotgun?" asked Billy.

The old warrior laughed and swung his mighty axe round his head till the blade flashed like a continuous band of steel and the air whistled at the cleavage of the sharp edge. Then he began to sing softly a war-song which may be roughly rendered in English thus:

> "At dawn I went out with my axe into the red fight;
> Like the grass before the fire, like the clouds before the wind,
> I drove them. I, Sikaso, I drove them.
> There were rivers that day; but the rivers were red.
> They were the rivers of the blood of my enemies;
> With my war-axe I killed them.
> This is the song of mighty Sikaso, and his terrible axe of death."

Although the boys of course did not understand the words, the fierce voice in which the old warrior intoned the chant made them realize what a terrible foe he was likely to prove in battle. But now as Sikaso brought his song to a conclusion and rested his axe on the ground, leaning on its hilt, he suddenly stiffened into an attitude of close attention.

"Hark, my white brothers!" he cried, "the war-eagles are gathering for the slaughter."

But the slight sound the keen ears of the savage had caught without difficulty was longer in making itself manifest to the two white boys. After a few minutes of listening, so intense as to be painful, they likewise, however, distinctly heard the regular, rhythmic dip of paddles coming down the river.

"There are six war canoes full of them," announced, Sikaso, with almost a groan, after he had given close attention to the sounds. "Alas, my white brothers, there is little use of our giving battle."

"Well, I for one am not going to give up without dropping a few of the cowardly wretches," cried Billy.

"Nor I," echoed Lathrop, enthused by Billy's brave example.

The old warrior's eyes kindled as he gazed at the two brave young Americans, each clutching his rifle and waiting for the moment to arrive when they could use them.

"If we only had had time to throw up a stockade, my brothers, we might have driven them off yet," he cried.

"Well, we'll give as good an account of ourselves as possible," declared Lathrop.

And now began what has been acknowledged to be the most trying part of any engagement, from a duel to a battle - the waiting for hostilities to begin. It seemed that an interminable time had elapsed from the moment that they heard the first "dip-dip" of the paddles to the sharp crack of a twig sounded in the jungle directly ahead of them. The snapped branch told them that the enemy's outposts were reconnoitering to see that the camp was actually, as it seemed to be, wrapped in sleep.

Apparently the scout, whoever he was, was soon convinced of the fact that the adventurers were slumbering, for he advanced boldly from the dark sheltering shadows of the jungle and emerged into the bright moonlight which flooded the clearing in which the camp stood.

Billy raised his rifle to his shoulder and the next minute would have been the savage scout's last had not old Sikaso sternly seized and lowered the weapon, saying in a tense whisper:

"The time is not yet ripe, my brother. To fire now would be unnecessarily to give the alarm. Wait until they are massed thick and then fire into the bodies of the Arab dogs."

The scout didn't waste much time in reconnoitering. After a short time spent in peering about he dived once more into the forest and Billy whispered to Lathrop:

"Now it's coming, old man."

And come it did.

Five minutes after the scout had dived back into the forest a dozen dark forms crept from the bush and stealthily advanced toward the tent.

The leader had reached the door and Billy was frantically imploring old Sikaso to let him shoot when an appalling shriek rent the air.

The old Krooman's axe flashed once in the moonlight and the leader of the attacking party lay dead at the tent door, severed almost to the chest.

There was not a second's time, however, to take in what had happened. In a flash the whole horde was upon them, and Billy and Lathrop began firing desperately into the mass of foemen who appeared to spring from every side of the clearing at once.

Even in this extremity a strange thought flashed across Billy's, mind:

"Where was Professor Wiseman?"

CHAPTER XII

IN THE HANDS OF SLAVE-TRADERS

The ebon form of the Krooman giant seemed everywhere at once.

In the moonlight his terrible axe flashed incessantly and every time it fell a shriek or a muffled groan showed that it had found its fatal mark. The huge form of the warrior black seemed, however, to bear a charmed life. Again and again one of the attacking force would fire at him, but the bullets seemed to be warded off by some supernatural force. He was immune alike to bullets and arrows - with which latter the natives attached to Muley-Hassan's force battled.

Billy and Lathrop fought with unflinching courage, pouring out a leaden hail into the onslaught that again and again seemed as if it must drive the attacking force back. But fighting at such desperately uneven odds could not in the nature of things last long. There came a minute when Billy, turning to reload, found that before he could snatch up a handful of cartridges a huge Arab was on top of him.

Lathrop's clubbed rifle struck the fellow helpless the next minute and sent his long, cruel knife with a ringing crash to the floor.

Before Billy's half breathed "Thanks, old man," had left his lips, however, another of Muley-Hassan's followers had rushed in and the moment would have been Lathrop's last but that Billy drove his fist into the fellow's face with a crashing blow that knocked him on the top of his fallen comrade. It was hand-to-hand fighting then with a vengeance. Billy seized hold of the muzzle of an Arab's revolver as it was thrust into his very face, and twisted it upward as it was discharged. Seizing up a camp chair Lathrop swung it round his head like a club and scattered the brains of a native follower of Muley-Hassan.

But strategy was to put an abrupt end to the fight even if it could have continued much longer.

Billy was bleeding from a cut over the forehead which blinded him, and Lathrop had got two nasty knife thrusts, one in the arm and the other in the fleshy part of the calf of his leg, when they were suddenly attacked from the rear by half-a-dozen slavers. The next minute, wounded and bound, they were as helpless as two captured puppies.

The fight was over, but the Arabs had come out of it with a badly crippled force.

Of the twenty-five men who had attacked the adventurers' camp ten had been killed outright and half a dozen others so badly wounded that they could not move. Hardly one of them had not received some minor injury, and the very fact that they had made such a poor showing against two American boys and a Krooman armed only with an axe, filled Muley-Hassan with savage rage.

Furiously the slave-dealer ordered the two boys brought before him. A huge fire had been lighted by his followers and in the glare cast by this he received them. It was a wild scene and the two boys hardly knew whether they were awake or dreaming, as they were roughly hustled into the presence of their captor.

Diego de Barros, his cruel, thin lips curled in a sneer that showed his yellow teeth, stood by the side of Muley-Hassan, the latter a tall determined-looking man with a crisp, curly black beard and a sinister cast of features. A long burnoose of white, worn after the Arab style, hung from his head and framed his dark features, which were just then overspread by a frown as black as thunder.

Outside the circle of firelight lay the bodies of the victims of the Krooman's axe and the boys' bullets. All who could do so of Muley-Hassan's followers were gathered about him, as the two young Americans were brought face to face with the man they had such good reason to fear.

"So these are the young Americans?" he asked as Billy and Lathrop returned his hawk-like gaze unflinchingly.

"No, sir," spoke up Diego, "they are not. Wiseman has just told me that the Chester boys have flown in their air-ship and these are the cubs left behind to guard the camp."

At Wiseman's name mentioned in such a connection both the boys started.

"What! they have gone?" thundered the Arab chief.

"Yes, sir," stammered Diego, his coward nature aroused at the sight of his superior's fury.

"And by this time they are rifling the ivory cache. That fool Wiseman shall pay dearly for this. Bring him to me," shouted the Arab.

Desperate as was the boys' position they could not restrain a start of amazement as Professor Wiseman, his face pale as ashes to his very lips, came tremblingly forward.

"You were attached to this boys' camp to prevent by all means their sailing till I attacked the camp and made them prisoners, were you not?" demanded Muley-Hassan angrily.

Wiseman stammered something in reply.

"You are a coward as well as a fool," went on the slave-dealer, a cruel sneer breaking over his face; "but you have blundered for the last time. Take this fool away and kill him!" he ordered, turning away as if there was an end of the business.

Pitiful cries broke from the lips of the unhappy professor as he heard his death-warrant thus pronounced. He threw himself on his knees and begged and pleaded in a loud screeching tone for a little more time. But the chief was obdurate.

"Take him away," was all he said, and his men, not daring to disobey his orders any longer, fairly dragged the unfortunate prisoner toward the river bank. There was a short, sharp scream that chilled every drop of blood in the boys' bodies and then a splash. Professor Wiseman had paid the price of his treachery.

It was not till long after that the boys heard the full measure of his villainy. How posing as a naturalist he had wandered up and down the Ivory Coast for years acting as the secret agent of Muley-Hassan and making arrangements for the smuggling of slaves and illicitly procured ivory out of the country. He was too accomplished a rascal to be suspected and his learned appearance made it still more improbable that he should be engaged in any illegal trafficking. It was small wonder, too, that he had started when Frank mentioned the name of Luther Barr, for it was Luther Barr whom he had betrayed to Muley-Hassan and advised him of the whereabouts of the wily old New Yorker's ivory cache. As soon as he heard Frank mention the name he had of course surmised that the pretended hunting expedition was merely a blind to cover a bold dash to recover the ivory, though how they were to discover its whereabouts he could not imagine till, by prying and listening, he learned that they had a map of the locality of the stolen stuff.

He had then dispatched native canoe-men to Muley-Hassan and apprised him of the coming of the boys, and Diego had been at once sent out by the Arab to secure possession of the map if possible and, failing that, to destroy the boys' canoes. That the aeroplane would also have been put out of commission there is little doubt, if Diego or Wiseman could have found an opportunity. The brutal Arab could then have disposed of the expedition at his leisure. But the Golden Eagle II was too closely guarded for the two spies to be able to harm it.

The Kroomen porters attached to the camp had, as old Sikaso had forecast, fled into the jungle at the first attack of the Arab's followers and they did not put in an appearance till long after the marauders had left the camp.

But what puzzled the boys, as they stood facing the Arab with Professor Wiseman's scream still ringing in their ears, was "What had become of the old warrior."

He could not have turned traitor. His valiant behavior in the skirmish made that impossible to consider a minute. But it was equally certain that he was nowhere to be seen. What could have become of him? A dread that he was dead oppressed both boys as they stood there waiting for the Arab to speak.

Muley-Hassan seemed to be considering.

He twisted the ends of his jet-black mustaches like a man lost in thought, and the firelight playing on his bold reckless features showed there an expression of deep perplexity. But it was no question of mercy that was agitating his mind.

It was whether he would kill the boys right there or sell them into slavery.

To his money-making mind the latter idea commended itself. Two strong youths such as they were would fetch a good price anywhere, and so it came about that Billy and Lathrop - who had fully expected to share the Professor's fate - were flung by no gentle hands into their bullet-riddled tent and left to pass the night as best they could. Two men were posted to watch them and a rough cuff on the head rewarded Billy's single attempt to speak to Lathrop.

The next day at dawn the camp was the scene of great activity. The dead were carried into the forest a short distance and buried, while the wounded were attended to with such rough surgery as Muley-Hassan knew. In this work Diego, his lieutenant, who seemed to be a sort of Jack-of-all-trades-outside of his regular occupation of scoundrel-aided him; bandaging the, cuts and extracting the bullets of his companions with some skill.

The boys were then given to eat some sort of stew in a big wooden basin and being just healthy American boys and not heroes of romance they ate heartily of the compound and felt better. Muley-Hassan himself examined the cut on Billy's forehead and Lathrop's two wounds and pronounced them mere scratches.

Just as it appeared that a start was about to be made the signal bell of the wireless rang. As our readers know it was Frank signaling from the Moon Mountains.

A sudden idea seemed to strike Diego at this. He called Muley-Hassan aside and talked earnestly with him for a few seconds, then he came up to the boy and demanded fiercely which one of them it was that understood wireless.

Lathrop replied that he did, and the next minute wished that he had bitten out his tongue before he had admitted it; for Diego, in a rough tone, ordered him to sit down at the instrument and reply that all was well at the River Camp.

"And, mind you, youngster - no tricks," he said

savagely, "or I'll kill you as dead as mutton. I understand the Morse code myself and can tell what you are sending; and send slow so that I can get every letter."

Lathrop was in a quandary. To refuse to sit down at the instrument meant instant death.

He could tell that by the look in Diego's eyes and from what he had seen of him he knew he would not stop at a little thing like a murder to drive home a point.

The question was, did the man really understand telegraphy? If he didn't and was only, bluffing Lathrop determined to inform Frank of the true state of affairs. Otherwise it would do neither himself nor the others any good to try to trick Diego.

With a prayer on his lips that the Portuguese might not have been stating the truth about his knowledge of wireless the boy started to send. He had in his mind the message he would try to get through:

"We have been attacked. Get help and follow us."

But he had hardly tapped out with a hesitating finger the first word of his message when he felt a bullet whiz by his ear and the report flashed so close to him that it deafened him and scorched his skin.

"Thought I was bluffing did you, eh?" sneered the Portuguese, "come now, no tricks; send out what I tell you or the next bullet will come closer."

And so it came about that the queer hesitating message that Frank received at Moon Mountains was sent out.

Immediately it was dispatched Muley-Hassan gave the order to advance and his ragged followers, carrying the worst wounded in improvised litters, set out toward the northwest.

"We are going to the Moon Mountains," whispered Billy to Lathrop, "at least it looks that way. I overheard Muley-Hassan say to Diego that we'd have to hurry to get the ivory - "

Lathrop's reply was cut short by a scene that sent the angry blood to both boys' faces.

Before the camp was abandoned for good and the plunge into the forest began, Muley-Hassan gave a sharp order and directed several of his men set about demolishing the camp. Diego himself smashed the field wireless of which Frank and Harry had been so proud. He hacked it to atoms with one of the heavy axes. The tents and provision boxes were next piled in a heap and set in a blaze.

As the column of dark smoke rose from the ruins of the once happy camp into the clear sky the order to advance was given and the train once more moved forward.

They had hardly deserted the clearing before, from the river bank, half a hundred wild figures appeared.

They were similar in appearance - only even more wild-looking than the savages fought off by Frank, Harry and Ben the previous day. Like the others their slashed and scarred faces and clay-daubed lips showed them to belong to one of the fierce cannibal tribes of the Bambara region.

Their leader, a tall, thin savage of exceptionally repulsive appearance, motioned with his fingers to his thick lips for absolute silence among his followers.

Clutching their great broad-headed war-spears the next moment the savages slipped into the forest in the direction the Arab and his band had gone. Steadily they advanced with the quiet stealthy tread of panthers on the track of their prey.

CHAPTER XIII

GORILLAS - AND AN AERIAL TOW-LINE

The mystery of the man on the hill bade fair to be an unsolved one, for although the boys watched for some time with considerable anxiety he did not reappear. This feature of the incident set them to comparing notes and they found that their impression of the apparition differed considerably. Both Frank and Harry were ready to swear that he was a black man, while Ben Stubbs was equally convinced that his skin was of a reddish hue. All three, however, agreed that he was weaponless so far as could be seen, and his attitude appeared to be more one of interested curiosity than of actual hostility.

"Well, there's no use wasting time in speculation," said Frank at last, "more especially as it does not look as if we can get any nearer to solving the problem in that way. The thing to do now is to get at the ivory and that as quickly as possible. If that man is the forerunner of a band that means to attack us, it is all the more reason that we should get a move on."

"Right you are, Captain," assented Ben, "and here goes!"

With a mighty swing of his pick the former prospector

dislodged a pile of the rough stones of which the cairn was composed and the boys, too, laid on with a will. In an hour or so all that was left of the once lofty cairn was a few big rocks.

Excitement ran fairly to fever heat as the last obstruction that lay between the adventurers and the ivory hoard was cast aside.

In a few minutes now, if all went well, they would be in possession of the treasure. More than once as they worked, Frank drew his field-glasses out of their case and scanned the surrounding wilderness of rocky chasms and swept the green jungle that lay stretched like an emerald ocean far below, but each time he replaced them with a sigh of relief. So far there was no sign of any rivals' approach, although Frank well knew that by this time Muley-Hassan must be upon his way to contest the boys' claim to the ivory.

As the last stone was chucked aside with a mighty heave by the combined forces the perspiring adventurers broke into a hearty cheer.

Beneath it was a wooden trap-door which had a ring placed in the middle evidently for the purpose of lifting it. Frank gave it a heft, but the weight was too much for even his wiry muscles; but when Ben and, Harry assisted him the door gave with a jump that threw them all to their feet.

Scrambling up in a second they rushed to the edge of the hole revealed by the uplifting of the wooden cover. What they saw showed them instantly that their wildest hopes had not been overdrawn. There, at their feet, lay a king's ransom in yellow ivory.

From the hole rose a fetid, sickening odor that at first was almost overpowering. It came from the rotting flesh that still adhered to the roots of many of the huge trunks.

With a cheer Harry was about to spring down into the aperture when Frank, with a quick exclamation, drew him back.

"Jump back for your life!" he shouted.

Harry was accustomed to obeying his brother in everything, and jump backward he did with an agility that would have done credit to a gymnast. Before he could ask a question Frank's revolver cracked and a little spit of dust shot up almost at his very feet.

There lay a tiny snake viciously wiggling about in its death agony, pierced through by Frank's bullet.

It was a rock adder - one of the deadliest of African snakes. Barely more than three inches in length, and a dull gray in color, it was small wonder that Harry in his excitement had not seen it as he was about to jump almost upon it.

"We shall have to be careful," said Frank, as he kicked aside the still writhing body of the disgusting looking reptile. "There is just a chance that Muley-Hassan, with the cunning of an Arab, may have put several more of those customers in here to guard his ivory."

It was therefore cautiously that the boys proceeded to work at getting the ivory out of the hole and although they killed three more of the venomous reptiles it seemed more probable that they had got in by accident than that the Arab slave-dealer had deliberately placed them there. By mid afternoon a big pile of ivory lay ready for transportation to the Golden Eagle Il and only a few more tusks remained in the hole.

"How are we ever going to get the tusks down the hill to the Golden Eagle II?" asked Harry as he gazed at the formidable pile.

"I have a better plan than that," replied Frank, "we will bring the Golden Eagle II here."

"What?" gasped both his listeners.

"Why not? It will be a ticklish job to land her on this spot, but I think I can do it. I mean to try anyhow."

"You are risking breaking up the ship," objected Harry.

"On the other hand, if we don't get this ivory out of here in jig time Muley-Hassan will be here with a big force and we shall assuredly all have our throats cut."

This argument proved insurmountable, and while Ben was left by the ivory Harry and Frank hurried down the steeps to the plateau on which they had left the Golden Eagle II. It was the work of a few minutes to tune her up. In a brief time from the moment they had left the ivory cache, considering the clamber they had had, the boys were in the air and headed for the spot where they had left the hoard.

But as they rose into the air they were startled by the sound of a shout and then another and another, then carne a volley of shots.

What could be the matter?

The shooting evidently was taking place at the spot where they had left Ben to guard the ivory.

Muley-Hassan! was the first thought that shot through Frank's brain.

The next minute, however, he dismissed the idea as absurd. The Arab, even by the swiftest marching, could not have reached the Moon Mountains in such record time unless he also had an air-ship, which Frank knew was impossible.

As the ship soared higher and rushed straight as an arrow through the air to the ivory cache a strange sight was revealed to the two young voyagers. High up on the mountain-side they could see Ben struggling with what appeared to be dozens of naked savages. The boys could see his gallant resistance as he swung his clubbed rifle again and again at his savage opponents. Several of them lay dead on the ground about him, but those that remained were attacking him with what seemed demoniacal fury.

"Good Lord," gasped Frank, "what on earth can have happened?"

"They're cannibals!" gasped Harry.

"No - no," exclaimed Frank hastily, "they're - give me the glasses quick, Harry - that's right - I thought so. They're not savages, but worse almost."

"What do you mean?"

"That they are gorillas!"

At her utmost speed the big aeroplane bore down on the scene of the unequal combat between Ben Stubbs and the savage beasts.

The boys could see that one of the brutes had seized their stalwart companion's rifle from him and with incredible strength had broken it in half as if it had been a wooden toy. The next minute Harry's rifle spoke and the gorilla that had just performed the miraculous feat of strength fell dead. With a shriek of rage the others turned to see whence came this new enemy.

At the sight of the great aeroplane bearing down upon them they at first started to flee with howls of terror, but the next minute they rallied and with low growls of rage, that bared their cruel fangs, they deliberately waited to see what this strange object might be.

This gave Ben a brief respite and he occupied it by reloading his revolver. The boys were delighted to see by this that their brave comrade was not seriously injured.

But now the Golden Eagle II was ready to settle and Frank, guiding his aerial steed with one hand, grasped his revolver with the other, for it was evident that the rush would come as they struck the ground. And come it did. As the wheels of the aeroplane struck the earth and Frank threw in the brakes sharply crashing into a rocky wall, with a howl of defiance the whole horde of man-like brutes rushed down on the air-craft with wicked rage in their spiteful little red eyes.

The leader of them, a huge "old man" gorilla, brandished an immense stone which he hurled with vicious energy at the new arrivals. Luckily it fell short of the air-ship or it would have crashed through the plane covers and have seriously crippled, if not ruined, the air-ship.

The boys' rifles cracked simultaneously and two of the attackers rolled over, with horrible human-like cries, but the leader, the bad "old man," was still in the field. As he saw his fellows fall he gave a mighty yell of rage and hatred that seemed to come from the depths of his hairy chest, and beating rapidly on it, as if it were a war-drum he rushed straight at the aeroplane.

"Don't let 'em get near the engines," was all Frank had time to shout before the avalanche of hairy, ill-smelling brutes was upon them. Some of them had armed themselves with rocks which they hurled with ferocious force. Others used nothing but their bare hands. Some of them, wounded as they were, fought with added fierceness. Desperately the boys fought them off and when the magazines of the rifles and revolvers were emptied they fell back on their hunting knives.

Frank had made a furious lunge at the "old man" and missed him by a hair's-breadth when he felt two great hairy arms encircle him from behind and the hot breath of one of his horrible opponents whistling savagely in his ear. He tried to lunge backwards at the creature, but toppled over and fell sprawling. In a flash the "old-man" gorilla was on him when Ben's revolver cracked and the "old-man," badly wounded, sprang high into the air and rolled over and over, clutching his head with both his huge hands and screaming in an agonized manner.

The fall of their leader seemed to discourage the others. They fought on for a while but it was half-heartedly. The boys had had time in the brief pause that followed the killing of the "old-man" to reload, and with their rifles newly charged they were in position to make terrible reprisals on the gorilla band for the mischief they had wrought. The monsters evidently were about to quit the battle when suddenly a cry rang through the air that ended the fight more abruptly than even the boys' bullets could have done.

"Ah-o-o-o-o-AH-O-O-O-O-o-o-o-o-o-o-o-o-o-o-o!"

It was the voice of the mountain once more.

With yells of dismay and terror the remainder of the gorilla band instantly dashed up the rocky mountain-side dragging with them, in grotesquely human fashion some of their wounded. Several of these, however, still lay on the ground and the boys put them out of their misery with a few well-directed shots. A pathetically human look lingered in the eyes of some of the injured gorillas and Harry burst out with:

"This is awful work. I'd rather fight a dozen bands of cannibals than have to do this."

"And yet," replied Frank, "if we hadn't killed them they'd have killed us."

At last the unpleasant work was over and the ivory was rapidly loaded into the aeroplane. But here an unanti-cipated difficulty manifested itself. Obviously the aeroplane would be too heavily laden if she attempted to carry all or even a good part of the ivory.

"Now we are stuck," cried Harry.

"Hold on," exclaimed Frank with a smile, "I anticipated this. We are going to turn the Golden Eagle into a tow-boat."

"A tow-boat?"

"That's what I said."

"What do you mean?"

Frank, in reply, bent over the stem-locker of the aeroplane and drew out what Harry instantly recognized as the silk envelope of an experimental dirigible they had built the year before.

"Now then," said Frank, "give a hand here."

They all three pulled and hauled till the envelope was spread level on the ground, all folds and creases having been carefully shaken out.

"Well," said Harry, "this would carry an awful weight of ivory, but how are you going to inflate it?"

"With these cylinders," was the answer as Frank opened the store-room below the floor of the Golden Eagle and pointed to a dozen cylindrical steel receptacles. "They contain more than enough pure hydrogen gas at a high pressure," he explained, "to inflate the bag."

In his enthusiasm Harry waved his helmet and Ben did

the same.

"An aerial express, hurray!"

The inflation hose was soon connected to the first of the cylinders and with a hiss the gas rushed into the bag when a turn of the wrench set free the precious stuff. Slowly the big yellow envelope swelled and assumed shape until by the time the last cylinder was empty it was tugging and straining to rise. But the boys had weighted it down with rocks and pegged its net ropes to the ground.

The ivory was loaded into a sort of rope basket, like those used to hoist cargo aboard a ship, and in a short time, so quickly did they work, they were ready for the air, so far as what Harry called "the airbarge" was concerned.

"We shall have to strip the Eagle," decided Frank, when the inflation job was finished.

"Of everything that we can spare," added Harry, setting to work at once to rip the transoms and detach the bolts that held the heavy wireless apparatus in place. As he did so, Frank was moved by a sudden thought.

"Hold on a second, Harry," he shouted, "I'll call up the river camp before we cut off all communication."
Rapidly he sent out the call. Again and again his nervous finger agitated the key - but there was no response.

"They - they don't answer," gasped Frank at last - heavy anxiety in his tones.

"Oh, Frank, do you think anything serious is the matter?" cried Harry.

"It may only be that the apparatus is out of order," replied the elder brother seriously; "but it looks bad. That field wireless was in prime condition and it would be next to impossible for them to fail to receive our call."

"Well, there is only one thing to be done," remarked the practical Ben Stubbs.

"And that is - ?" queried Harry.

"To get back there as soon as possible, for if they need us they need us dern bad," was the energetic reply.

Half an hour later the Golden Eagle, stripped of all her heavy gear and only carrying just enough gasoline to get her to the river camp, where the adventurers expected to find a reserve supply, rose slowly into the air with her queer tow tugging behind on the wireless ground rope. The boys had cached the wireless apparatus and the other gear, to be called for at some more opportune time. To their great regret, also, they had had to leave some of the ivory behind them. But the majority of what they did not dare trust to the gas-bag they carried in the chassis. Luckily for them there was hardly a breath of wind and the novel carrier towed well.

As the occupants of the great aeroplane gazed back at the sinister Moon Mountains as they fast faded out - they saw silhouetted against the evening sky a dark figure.

It was recognized at once as one of the beaten gorillas scouting to see if the terrible white men had really gone.

"There's the man we saw this afternoon," laughed, Frank, as with rapidly beating propellers the Golden Eagle II winged her way with the convoy toward the River Camp.

CHAPTER XIV

AN ESCAPE - AND WHAT CAME OF IT

From the pace at which Muley-Hassan's band traversed the jungle paths it was evident to the two young captives that there was imperative need in Muley-Hassan's mind of arriving somewhere at a set time. The usual noonday rest, which even the avaricious slave-trader was in the habit of taking, was not observed and the travelers pressed straight on. Lathrop and Billy were almost ready to drop with fatigue when that evening, just at dusk, they arrived at the bank of a muddy river which Muley-Hassan, impatient as he was to proceed, decided it would be unwise to ford till daylight - when they could look for a good crossing place. At the spot which they had halted, the stream - swollen apparently by rains in the mountains - roared between its banks, in a dark chocolate-colored flood.

Muley-Hassan himself was the only one of his band provided with a tent, or anything resembling one, and the boys shared the common bed of the rest of the party - which was the ground. A more unwholesome resting-place in Africa, particularly on the steamy, swampy banks of a river, could hardly be imagined. So indeed Muley-Hassan seemed to think, for after a short time, during which the boys vainly tried to secure some sleep, he ordered Diego to provide them with blankets to place between themselves and the bare earth.

"I expect to get a good price for them eventually," he said, "and I don't want to lose them unless I have to."

As the boys' wrists and ankles were bound with tough grass while there was no particular attempt made to watch them, and soon the snores of the camp bespoke that it was at rest. Then it was that Billy whispered to Lathrop.

"Now's our time to try for it!"

"Try for what?" whispered back Lathrop in an inert tone.

"To get away."

"What!"

"I mean it. I found a sharp stone imbedded in the ground near to me and I have nearly sawed through my wrist-bands."

After a few seconds' more vigorous scraping against the stone, Billy whispered:

"My hands are free. Wait till I wiggle my fingers and get up some circulation and then we'll make our attempt - "

When he had once more got full control of his cramped fingers Billy stooped cautiously over and loosened the thongs about his ankles. So tightly had they been drawn, though, that it took some little time to get the cramps out of them. At last, however, the boy succeeded in restoring the circulation and then he was ready for the most daring step of his attempt. Cautiously he fell on his hands and knees and began to crawl toward the nearest of the sleeping slave-traders.

"What are you going to do, Billy?" asked Lathrop, in an agony of fear lest the man should awaken.

"Watch me," was the young reporter's reply, as on his stomach he wiggled painfully across the few yards separating him from the sleeping man. In reality it took only a few minutes, but to both the boys the period of time occupied seemed interminable.

But it was no time to hurry things. One false step night cost them their lives and Billy realized this.

With the slow deliberate movement of a snake he, reached out his hand when he got near enough and took from the sleeping man's side his long curved Arab scimitar. Then he glided back to Lathrop as silently as he had left.

He had just reached his resting-place when there was a stir from the further side of the camp. Like a rabbit ducking into its hole Billy was under his blanket and apparently fast asleep in a second. But his heart beat so loudly that it felt to him that anyone who was not deaf could hear it a hundred yards away.

The man who had moved was Diego and the boys could hear his cat-like footfalls as he neared their sleeping-places. Once he stumbled over one of the sleeping men and the aroused one rose with a start and called wildly:

"What is it?"

"Hush, Adab," cautioned Diego, "it is I - Diego. I'm going to give an eye to those two American brats."

"They're tied up hard and fast enough," chuckled the other.

"If they were of any other nationality - yes;" was Diego's reply, "but these Yankees are brave and clever enough to escape from almost any trap."

"You bet we are," thought Billy to himself, giving a realistic snore.

Although he did not dare to open his eyes, the young reporter could feel Diego standing over them in the moonlight and gazing down at them to ascertain if they were still "hard and fast," as the other had expressed it.

For an instant a terrible thought flashed across Billy's brain.

"Suppose Diego should take an idea to examine their thongs?"

But the lieutenant of Muley-Hassan apparently was satisfied, for after a few minutes' scrutiny he turned to go Billy could hear his feet scrape as he swung around.

At almost the same instant the night was filled with savage cries and the camp was thrown into confusion by an onrush of wild figures before whose spears the half-awakened Arabs were slaughtered like sheep.

Not realizing in the least what was happening, Billy

yet conjectured that the Arabs were just then too busy to pay any attention to himself and Lathrop. With two slashes of the stolen scimitar he severed Lathrop's bonds and dragging him to his feet dived into the forest.

As they entered its recesses a fleeing Arab, still clutching his rifle, dashed by them and an instant later fell dead. He had been speared through the back.

Billy, with a quick inspiration, seized the dead man's long rifle and his ammunition pouch and, followed by the bewildered Lathrop, plowed desperately forward into the screen of the jungle.

Behind them they heard cries for mercy and fierce shouts from the attacking savages. At first the cries and imprecations of the slave-traders predominated and then, by the altered sounds that came from the scene of the fighting and the crashing of the Arabs' volleys, the boys realized that the tide of battle had changed and that the Arabs were driving back the attacking force.

"What do you suppose happened, Billy?" asked Lathrop, only half awake, as the boys, with the fleetness and endurance that desperate need lends, plunged deeper and deeper into the forest.

"Why, that some cannibal tribe that Muley-Hassan pillaged for slaves at some time has trailed him and attacked him," hazarded the reporter.

How near he came to the truth our readers know. The band that had made the midnight attack was the same that had painstakingly trailed Muley-Hassan since he destroyed the boys' camp on the river bank.

"But the Arabs have beaten them off?" queried Lathrop.

"Evidently," replied Billy, as the volleys died out and victorious Arab shouts were beard. "Hark at that! It's really too bad. I'd like to have seen old Muley and his precious band driven into the river. But if they have driven off the savages they'll be thinking about chasing us."

As he spoke there came a low, growling sound that seemed to proceed from some distance, but nevertheless filled the air. It rumbled and rolled above them like -

"Thunder!" exclaimed both boys in the same breath.

"We've got to find shelter of some kind, quick," exclaimed Billy; "these tropical storms are unlike our little disturbances, and if we get caught among these trees in one, of them we stand a good chance of being killed. It looks like we've jumped out of the frying-pan into the fire."

Without the least idea in which direction they were proceeding, the two chums struggled bravely on, Billy encouraging the flagging Lathrop from time to time with a joke, though these latter were, as Billy admitted to himself:

"Pretty dismal!"

At length, just as dawn was beginning to break, they found themselves facing a steepish cliff of rough rocks.

"Well, here's where we turn back," remarked Billy,

bitterly discouraged nevertheless.

If they were lost in this equatorial forest, what chance did they stand of ever seeing their home and friends again?

As for Lathrop he sat down on a rock overgrown with a kind of monstrous lichen and gave way to tears. But not for long. Lathrop was a plucky enough lad, and as Billy truthfully remarked:

"We are going to have enough water before long without our turning on the weeps."

So Lathrop braced up and the boys looked about them. To their intense joy they soon spied in the rocks, a short distance from where they then were, a dark hole partly overgrown by creepers, which was evidently the entrance to a cavern. At the same instant there began a mighty pattering on the leaves of the dense tropic growth all about them, and a louder growl of thunder announced that the storm that had been heralded a few hours before was about to break.

"Well, me for that African Waldorf-Astoria," cried Billy, grasping his rifle and making a dive for the hole. Lathrop followed him and as soon as they were inside the cave he lit a match from his waterproof box.

"Looks to me like there might be snakes in here," he whispered, awed by the darkness and silence of the place.

"Rats," laughed Billy, although he himself felt by no means sure that at any moment some scaly monster might not descend from the roof; "but I'll tell you what we'll do. Light a fire."

"How are we to get wood?" asked the practical Lathrop.

"There's plenty of it right at the mouth of the cave. I'll get a few armfuls and in a minute we'll have things snug."

The young reporter hastened to the cave mouth and in a few trips had gathered up several huge armfuls of wood-drift of all kinds from under the great trees all about. He was just re-entering the cave when there came a flash of blinding light so brilliant that it seemed as if the sky itself had split wide open. A bluish glare enveloped the forest and the lightning flash was instantly followed by a crash of thunder that shook the ground under the boys' feet.

"Well, they don't do things by halves in this country," remarked Billy as he re-entered the cave after a second of being temporarily stunned by the terrific flash.

It didn't take the boys long to have their wood in a blaze and as the smoke did not, as they had feared, fill the cavern, they assumed that there must be some opening above through which it escaped. This fact they verified shortly when, after the storm had been waxing in fury for half-an-hour, a perfect torrent of water came tumbling in from the rear of the rocky cavern.

"Hark!" exclaimed Billy as the boys busied themselves trying to scrape out a water-course that would divert the flood from their fire. From far in the rear of the cave came a plaintive sound of "Mi-ou, Mi-ou."

"Cats!" cried Lathrop.

"Cats nothing," was Billy's scornful reply; "here, let's have a look."

He seized a blazing brand out of the fire and hastened to the place from which the sounds emanated.

"Come here, quick, Lathrop," he cried. The younger lad scurried back and found Billy bending over a roughly constructed nest or bed. On it lay four tiny, fuzzy yellow things. They were "meowing" at the tops of their voices as the torrent of water that had annoyed the boys dripped into their snug nesting-place. At the same instant the boys became aware of a sickening odor of decaying flesh.

"Come on! we've got to get out of here quick as quick as we can," exclaimed Billy as they hastened towards the fresh air.

"Why, what is it, Billy?" asked Lathrop.

"I don't know; but I think that those are lion cubs - they look like the ones I've seen in the Bronx Zoo," was the young reporter's reply, "and if they are, this is no place for us. Come on - the storm is letting up. Let's get out quick before the old ones get back."

The storm, with the suddenness with which these furious tropical disturbances arise and vanish, had indeed gone and the sun was shining down once more on the drenched jungle, which glittered with diamond like spangles as the rays struck the dripping fronds and branches. But the boys had no eyes for the scene about them, beautiful as it was, for as they emerged from the cave a low growl greeted them.

Crouched on the ground - her tail lashing the earth like a cat's when it is about to spring - was a huge tawny lioness - her cruel green eyes fixed full upon them.

CHAPTER XV

THE FLYING MEN

For a breath the boys stood petrified and then Billy hastily slipped a cartridge into the rifle he had taken from the dead slave-trader. But even as he did so the lioness curved her lithe body, as if her backbone had been a steel spring, and launched her great form through the air.

That minute would have been Billy's last - for in his excitement he pulled the trigger before he had brought the rifle to his shoulder and the bullet whistled harmlessly into the air - but for a strange thing that now occurred.

While the tawny brute was in mid-spring, her cruel claws outspread to maul the unhappy reporter, a great spear whizzed straight at her and buried itself in her heart just behind the left shoulder. With a howl of pain the brute fell short in her spring and, before she could make another attack, Billy had reloaded and sent a bullet crashing between her eyes. As the lioness rolled over dead, the tall form of a. savage sprung out of the jungle and stood for a second gazing at the boys, as much astonished, it seemed, at them as they were at him.

Captain Wilbur Lawton

Billy, seeing that the best plan was to be pacific, threw down his rifle and cried:

"Seesenab," (peace); the word be recollected hearing the big Krooman use the day that he attempted to take his unlucky photographs.

"Seesenah - white boys," replied the other, the latter words in fair English and in a deep guttural tone, coming forward with the head of his other spear held downward in token of peace. "From where come the white boys - what do they in our land?" was his next question.

"We are lost," explained Billy, "and we are also, blamed hungry," he added, in a burst of confidence.

The savage smiled and rubbed his stomach.

"That's the idea," cried the irrepressible reporter. "Heap - empty - savee?"

The man leant over the dead lioness and, using his spear-point as a skinning knife, rapidly stripped her of her hide. Then, swinging the pelt over his shoulder he motioned to the boys to follow him.

"I don't know where the dickens he means to take us," confided Billy to Lathrop as they obediently trailed along behind, "but so long as we get something to eat I'm so hungry that I don't care if we get eaten the next minute."

"That's just the way I feel," agreed Lathrop, "and anyhow he seems to be a pretty decent sort. He saved your life, that's one thing sure."

"I guess I'll never make a mighty hunter," said Billy dolefully, "there was a chance to make real Bwana Tumbo shot and I missed it."

The savage stalked along in front of them for some distance till they suddenly emerged on a small clearing by a river bank, in which a rough native camp had been pitched. The tents of grass occupied by the hunters being of a peculiar conical shape, like the pointed caps that used to be labeled "Dunce."

Much excitement was created by the arrival of the two boys and their companion, and the hunters crowded round the chums while their guide explained with a wealth of gesture the incident of the killing of the lioness, and also the fact that the boys were very hungry.

Several of the men instantly filled wooden bowls with something from a pot that simmered over the fires and the bowls were thrust before the two ravenous boys. As there were no forks of course the boys used their fingers. But this did not interfere with their appetite and after they had put away two bowls apiece the savages' opinion of them evidently rose considerably. Among the West African natives a big eater is esteemed as a mighty man. Lathrop was considerably embarrassed, however, while he satisfied his hunger by the attention the hunters bestowed on his red hair. Several of them came up behind him and rubbed their hands in it as if they imagined it possessed some sort of medicinal value. Had any one at home dared to take such liberties with the boy's rubicund locks there would have been a fight right away, but Lathrop felt that the best policy to assume in the present situation was silence, and as the old ship captain said to his mate, "dem little of that."

"I say, Billy," whispered Lathrop suddenly, as, after eating the stew, they watched the hunters piling their belongings into their canoes, "you don't suppose they mean to fatten us up to eat us, do you?"

"Well, we can't starve even if that is the reason," replied the practical Billy, "but so far they seem friendly enough. They have not even taken my rifle away."

"That looks encouraging, certainly," replied Lathrop; "if only we knew where Frank and Harry and good old Ben were we might find this all very interesting, as it is though - "

"We've got to make the best of it," chimed in Billy, "come on. See old job-lots is signing to us to come down and get in a canoe."

"Whatever they mean to do with us they seem determined to make us comfortable," remarked Billy, as the boys took their seats in a canoe in which skins had been piled to make an easy seat.

For most of that afternoon they paddled steadily up the brown river, the savages singing from time to time an unending sort of chant, that sounded like nothing so much as a continuous repetition of:

"I-told-you-so. I-told-you-so. I - told-YOU-SO."

"Hum," commented Billy, "if anyone had told me so I'd have stayed in New York."

At length after what seemed endless hours of paddling and chanting the river took an abrupt turn and the boys found themselves at the foot of a steep cliff that towered up, it seemed, for six hundred feet at least. It was formed of black basalt and was crowned with a fringe of contrasting vegetation, but the most remarkable thing about it was that its surface was literally honeycombed with small holes from which, as the canoe cortege drew up, innumerable heads were poked.

An astonishing thing, however, about the men who scrutinized the lads from their lofty watch-towers, was that they were several degrees lighter in complexion than the boatmen and almost as white as the boys in fact. Their features, too, were different. As the boys looked in wonderment at this extraordinary dwelling-place and its equally strange inhabitants, Billy gave an excited shout:

"Great jumping horn-toads, look at that!"

One of the light-colored men had emerged from his, hole and with as little concern as if he were taking a walk had suddenly launched himself into space. But instead of falling to the ground or into the river, as the boys had fully expected to see him do, he floated gracefully to the opposite bank of the river with as little effort as a settling bird.

"Good land of hot-cakes, Lathrop, do you realize where we are?" almost shrieked the excited Billy.

"In the village of the Flying Men," stammered Lathrop, as, one after another, the inhabitants of the rock holes dropped from their aeries and floated groundwards. As the boys watched they saw distinctly that each man, from his wrist to his side, was possessed of a sort of leathery fiber like that of bat's swing, and that as their arms were of unusual length this fiber supported them in their downward flights like a parachute.

"I'll never call any one a liar again as long as I live," choked out Billy, as one after another these strange beings gathered in a chattering group on the river bank.

"But they can't fly upward," exclaimed Lathrop, pointing eagerly to where some of the gliders, having swum the river, were nimbly clambering up a grass rope-ladder to their homes.

"Oh, gee! if I only had a camera," groaned Billy.

"It will be no use telling anyone about this even if we do get out of here, they'll say that we have had a rarebit dream."

"That's so," assented Lathrop, "and honestly, Billy, are you sure we are awake?"

"Sure," replied the reporter giving himself a vicious pinch, and exclaiming "Ouch!"

But there was no time to talk further. Their guide now came up to them and jumping into their canoe paddled them to where the end of the rope-ladder dangled in the stream. He pointed upward for them to ascend. But Billy's curiosity would not let him mount before he had asked a question.

"Who are these people?" he asked in, for him, an awed tone.

"Very old-time people," rejoined their guide. "We hunt for them, work for them. They the same as fetish.'"

The boys mounted the ladder slowly.

Unused as they were to such a contrivance it required all their nerve to keep on going up, as they swung at a higher and higher altitude above the river. Neither of them dared to look down, as they were certain that they would be overcome by dizziness.

With their eyes glued to the rock in front of them, they mounted what seemed to be endless rungs till at last they found themselves at the top of the ladder and facing a large opening cut in the rock.

As they found out later, this was the main entrance to the dwelling of this strange community and from it various galleries and passages branched off to their separate dwelling-places. Each family lived in a rock house exactly adapted to the size of the circle. There were six stories, so to speak, of these dwelling-places, but they all communicated, either by means of stair-ways cut in the rock or inclined galleries, with the main passage at the entrance of which the chums now stood.

Their guide, who was immediately behind them on the swaying ladder, took the lead as soon as the three stood side by side on the summit, and escorted them down the long passage. Before they started he took from a bracket in the wall a kind of torch, made of some resinous wood unfamiliar to the boys. Striking piece of flint against his spear blade he soon produced light and holding the torch high above his head, so that its light shone on the walls, rendered glossy by the rub of uncounted ages of greasy elbows and bodies, he led the way down the passage. The boys could feel that after walking a short distance it took a sudden rise and yet further a cool wind began to blow in their faces.

About a hundred yards from the spot where they first noticed the air stirring in their hair the boys and their guide emerged on a scene whose beauty at first shock almost took the lads' breath away.

Before them stretched a fertile valley neatly divided into patches - each hedged off in squares in which flourished all sorts of vegetables, including sweet corn and potatoes and several other less familiar varieties. In pastures, fenced in with mathematical regularity by hedges of the African cactus thorn, herds of humped cattle were feeding contentedly in the mellow glow of the setting sun, occasionally lowing softly, which latter made Billy, as he expressed it, "long for the old farm."

The Winged Men likewise cultivated, it seemed, fruits of many kinds and had also stockades in which poultry, of breeds strange to the boys, but undoubtedly sprung from the aboriginal African fowl, were abundant.

It seemed as if they had struck a land in which the inhabitants lived an ideal life, surrounded as they were by every comfort and necessity that one could imagine; but that even they were distressed by the raids of enemies transpired when the boys' guide, whose name they had learned by this time was Umbashi, pointed to the west in which the setting sun was now kindling a ruddy glow and said:

"Sometime elephant come - then much trouble."

Of the full significance of those words, however, neither boy dreamed as, after a supper of fresh corn, bitter melon, stewed deer meat and a dessert formed of some sort of custard they sank to sleep on their couches of skins, spread for them by Umbashi's direction in a vacant dwelling in the cliff face.

Their slumber senses carried them back to New York and Billy was in the midst of escorting Umbashi in full war paint through the office of the New York Planet, followed by hordes of joshing reporters and inquisitive office boys, who wanted to know whether he'd match his dusky friend to fight Jim Jeffries, when he was awakened by Umbashi himself, who in a few words told him it was morning and time to get up and dress swiftly, as the King of the Flying Men wanted to see him and his young companion at once.

CHAPTER XVI

FOOLING AN ARAB CHIEF

"Frank, what do you make of it?"

"Harry, I don't know what to think."

"Ain't nuffin fer it but ter keep on hopin' fer the best, as the feller said when they had a rope around his neck fer horse-stealing and was about to string him up."

The three - Frank and Harry Chester and Ben Stubbs - were standing round the charred remains of their once lively, well-equipped camp - where they had arrived that morning at daybreak after a tiresome night spent circling about in the moonlight trying to locate it - and now the reason why they had failed to see the white tents was fully apparent by their blackened sites.

"Billy and Lathrop have been carried off!" It was Harry who spoke.

"Beyond a doubt. I thought at first that the raid must have been made by cannibals, but cannibals do not carry rifles, as a rule, and look here." Frank stooped and picked up half-a-dozen cartridges of the kind used by the Arab slave-traders.

"You know there were no shells like that in our party," he went on, "but I can see by the collection of empty shells in the place where the tent stood that Billy and Lathrop must have put up a hot defense."

"Frank, do you - you don't think, do you - " Harry burst out.

"That they have been killed?" Frank finished for him. "No, I do not. Unless they fell in the fight and then we should have seen their bodies down with the others by the river. No, it is my idea that they have been carried off to be sold as slaves. They would have a high market value you know."

Harry groaned.

"But don't you think there is a chance of our getting them back?"

Frank's face grew grave.

"Of course we are going to try every means in our power, but once in the hands of that scoundrel Muley-Hassan it is doubtful if we ever see them again. There is only one thing for us to do."

"And that is -?"

"To get back to the Moon Mountains at once. But we have no gasoline."

This was a stunning blow; in the excitement their of fuel had not occurred even to the farseeing Frank. They had had, as our readers know, to leave most of their gasoline at the Moon Mountains in order to lighten the aeroplane. Without it they could not move an inch in their air-craft. Harry tested the tank. Only a few paltry gallons remained - not enough to drive the aeroplane ten miles.

As the boys stood, struck dumb by the realization of the disaster that had overtaken them, Ben Stubbs, who had been down to the river bank, reappeared.

"Look here!" he exclaimed, holding out at arms length a long white cloak. One glance at the garment was enough - it was an Arab article of dress. There was no further doubt about it, then. Muley-Hassan and his men had carried off Billy and Lathrop.

"But that's not the most extraordinary part of it," went on Ben; "while there are half a dozen of the Arabs' canoes down there, there are a lot of others, that must have belonged to a bunch of natives from their shiftless look - and I could see the bare imprint of the savages' feet in the mud, coming after the Arabs had trod around there."

This was a new mystery. Apparently, then, a tribe of cannibals had been on the trail of the Arabs who had carried off their two young companions. This could only mean one thing, that they meant to punish the Arab slave-dealers for some outrage and, while this would have been quite satisfactory to the boys under other conditions, as things were it meant that there would be a fight in which both Lathrop and Billy would probably be seriously wounded, if not killed. How wrong this surmise was we know, and it serves to show how very wide of the mark it is possible for the constructors of a theory to steer.

And here for a time we will leave our despairing friends while we go back to the Moon Mountains.

The outline of the Golden Eagle II, in her flight to the river camp, had not faded out on the twilight sky, before, through the jungle at the foot of the Moon Mountains, a strange figure pushed its way. It was Sikaso, but a changed Sikaso from the agile muscular black who had wielded his axe with such terrible effect at the fight of the evening before. His ebony body was cut and scarred with the signs of his battle with the thorns and saw-bladed grasses of the dense forest, across which he had cut in desperate haste, scorning all paths in order to warn the Boy Aviators and their chum Ben of the rapid approach of Muley-Hassan. With that strange instinct that white men in Africa recognize in certain of the natives as a sixth sense, the giant black had read in a fire kindled after the battle, that the boys were at that moment in the Moon Mountains, and had at once set out - exhausted as he was - at top speed on the long journey. Only a man of his adamantine strength could have endured the hardships and it had fatigued even his iron frame, as was evident by his stumbling footsteps as he made his way up the side of the mountain - pausing from time to time as if to listen to the whisperings of his mysterious instinct.

Billy and Lathrop, half inclined to accuse the old black in their minds of base desertion, did him a gross injustice. After he had seen the two boys taken prisoners, the old warrior had realized that he could be of far more use to them at liberty than he would be if made captive by Muley-Hassan. Indeed there was no doubt in his own mind that the Arab would put him to death instantly if he ever got his hands on him. He had therefore built a fetish fire and in it had made out distinctly Frank and Harry and Ben in their air-ship, encamped on the mountain-side, and had set out without delay at the peculiar jog-trot by which the native bush-runners can cover daily as much ground, and more, than a horse.

But the huge Krooman was doomed to as bitter a disappointment as the youths he was in search of had experienced at their return to the river camp. He found the spot on which the Golden Eagle had rested deserted, but still urged on by his strange sense of locality he finally stumbled upon the ivory cache.

"Um, big fight here," he mused to himself as he gazed about him at the mangled bodies of the gorillas which showed black as ink on the rocks in the sharp, brilliant moonlight. The heap of uncollected ivory was the next thing to attract his eye and with a guttural grunt the negro helped himself to a drink of water from his skin-bag while he sat down to ponder. He did not waste much time in reflection. Springing to his feet he vanished down one of the dark recesses of the mountain-side and was gone about an hour. When he returned he picked up an armful of the ivory - a load that would have staggered three ordinary men - and, hefting it easily in his arms, vanished with it into the dark shadows. For two hours he worked steadily and at the close of that period there was not enough ivory left about the cache to make a watch-charm of. Old Sikaso had found a new hiding place for the stuff the boys were compelled to leave.

Then he sat himself once more down on the rock, and leisurely smashing to pieces with his inseparable axe, the wooden cover that had been over the cache, he selected, with a good deal of care one of the dead gorillas. Having found the one that seemed to suit him; he cut off from its flank a hunk of meat with his keen weapon and producing a flint and steel soon had the meat toasting over a blaze. When it was done to his satisfaction he leisurely ate it and washed it down with a draught from his skin-bag. He then cooked several more pieces of gorilla meat which he tucked in his waist-band, and shouldering his axe and humming to himself his grim war-song, he set out at the same swinging dog-trot on his long trip to the river bank. With the vitality common to such men, his brief rest and refreshment had rendered his tired frame as vigorous as ever and there was no trace of fatigue in the steady trot of the ebony figure as it plunged into the dark forest and vanished.

A second later, however, the figure reappeared as a noise of voices was heard drawing nearer down a forest trail. Throwing himself on his face and lying as motionless as a fallen log, the Krooman watched as Muley-Hassan and his followers - almost worn out and sadly diminished in numbers since their fight with the boys and with the cannibals - appeared. True, they had beaten the latter off, but at great loss to themselves, and the few men that now limped forward - urged on only by the fierce voice of Diego and Muley-Hassan - appeared ready to drop in their tracks from exhaustion.

"A hundred pounds of ivory to every man of you if we get there before they have cleaned the place out," the Arab was shouting by way of encouraging his men. Old Sikaso, with a grim chuckle, watched them make their way up the mountain-side and then laughed softly to himself as their imprecations of rage and fury broke out as they reached the cache - and found it empty!

Somewhat cheered by the vigorous Ben, who proposed to paddle down the river to the nearest settlement himself the next day, if some news were not heard of Billy and Lathrop, the boys were preparing for bed that evening - the bed consisting of the floor of the Golden Eagle's stripped cabin - when they were startled by Ben holding up a warning finger.

"Hark!" he exclaimed eagerly.

The boys listened.

"There's somebody coming," were Ben's next words.

Sure enough drawing closer every minute they could hear a soft patter-patter coming down a jungle-trail and evidently, by the sound, heading for the camp.

"Who can it be?" exclaimed Frank in a low tone, not daring even to mention the wild hope that surged in his heart. For a minute he thought that it might be the missing chums, and that even Harry and, to a less degree, Ben, shared his thought he saw by their parted lips and tensely strained eyes.

In absolute silence they listened as the footfalls drew in toward them, but not by even the wildest stretch of the imagination could they make out more than one man's footsteps.

Instinctively each member of the party raised his revolver as the bushes parted and from them tottered a man who was very evidently in the last stages of exhaustion. The figure staggered forward to the aeroplane as the boys and Ben lowered their revolvers, seeing that, whoever the newcomer was there was no fear of violence from him. It was Ben who recognized him first:

"Sikaso!" he cried, as the figure crumpled up in a heap, completely exhausted.

The boys rushed to the fallen man's side as they heard the name. They bathed the huge black's head with water and after a few minutes he opened his eyes and recognized them with a faint smile. After he had been given some nourishment he completely recovered from his spell of weakness which be called:

"Big fool - all same woman," quite omitting to state that he had traveled almost eighty miles since the preceding midnight.

The boys sat late listening to what the black had to tell of the attack on the camp - of Professor Wiseman's treachery and death - and of the carrying off of the boys. Then Sikaso went on to gleefully relate, while they warmly clasped his mighty hands, how he had hidden the rest of the ivory and how he had seen Muley-Hassan pass on his way to the rifled hiding place.

"But Billy and Lathrop, Sikaso, tell us quick, were they with Muley-Hassan?"

The black shook his head slowly.

"No see Four-Eyes - no see Red Head," he said sorrowfully.

The last ray of hope concerning the fate of the two young adventurers seemed to have been extinguished.

CHAPTER XVII

THE "ROGUE" ELEPHANT

In the meantime Billy and Lathrop, having been introduced to the chief, were making themselves very much at home in the village or cliff colony of the Flying Men. The morning after the day of their arrival a hunting expedition was organized by their new-found friend and in company with a dozen or more of the Flying Men, and the ordinary natives, who seemed to occupy the position of inferiors to their winged masters, the expedition set out.

They crossed the fields and garden patches that the boys had observed the evening before and, after traversing a few miles of swampy ground overgrown with a tough yellow grass, they plunged into a forest of mahogany and silk cotton trees.

It was while crossing the expanse of yellow grass at Billy performed a feat that caused all of them to hold him as a mighty hunter. They had been pushing their way along a narrow trail with the tops of the vegetation waving a good three feet above their heads, when there was a sudden grunt heard ahead and the noise of great rushing through the wiry grass.

"Big pig," announced the boys' friend as the others got

their spears ready to cast. Billy and Lathrop in their eagerness plunged on ahead of the others - Lathrop with a small spear and his revolver - which by the way was useless, he having expended all his cartridges - and Billy with the Arab rifle. Suddenly from dead ahead of the two boys there was a savage squeal and, before either of them realized what had happened, a boar with gleaming white tusks and bristly hair rushed out of the tangle and squarely charged them.

Lathrop went down before his furious onslaught and in his fall carried Billy to the ground with him. In another moment both boys would have been badly gored, perhaps killed, had not the reporter, in the very instant that the boar with wickedly gleaming little red eyes turned to attack Lathrop with his fierce tusks, raised himself on one arm and fired. The bullet struck their assailant full in the ear and penetrated the brain. With a surprised squeal he turned and ran a few feet and then dropped dead. The rest of the hunting part came up at this moment and Billy received warm congratulations - which, as he did not understand, meant as much as most of such felicitations.

It was not long after this incident that the plunge into the cool darkness of the forest began. The men went warily - as if expecting to be attacked at any moment - and the boys, on inquiring of their guide the reason for this caution, only received the reply that elephant tracks had been seen and that as a "rogue" elephant had lately been doing great damage to the crops of the cliff-dwellers they were anxious to kill him if possible.

A rogue elephant is one that has become estranged from the rest of his kind by reason of his fierce intractability. He is in fact what in the west is described, in speaking of a horse, as "loco" or crazy. Such animals - they are generally males - are extremely dangerous to hunt and are generally given a wide berth. They are mischievous in the extreme, moreover, and do great damage, seemingly wantonly, to any crops or garden patches that they may find in their neighborhood. Usually the natives are too terrified to offer any resistance and placidly allow the animal to devastate to the bent of his will. The cliff dwellers, however, had suffered so much from the depredations of this particular animal that they were determined to drive him out of their neighborhood, and that was the real purpose of the hunting party.

"Well, it looks as if we are in for a good exciting morning of it," remarked Billy as they trudged along beneath trees that shot up to unknown heights with great rope-like creepers dangling from their upper branches, looking like ladders leading up into "Jack in the Beanstalk-land." Occasionally a patch of blue could be sighted through the tree-tops, but for the most part the hunters progressed along the floor of the forest under a regular roof of greenery. There was plenty of life in this tipper story of the earth jungle. Troops of monkeys with chattering and gesticulations swung from bough to bough and looked in wonder on the invaders of their realm and then, taking imaginary fright, galloped off through the tree-tops in panic, only to stop a little distance further on and throw down fruit or bits of stick at the men below them. Gorgeous birds, too, flitted about like jewels seen in a setting of green velvet, while underfoot there was no lack of life either. Strange insects, shaped like sticks or leaves or even bits of moss, attracted the attention of the alert boys although they passed over hundreds of such nature mimics unnoticed, owing to the perfection of their mimicry.

At last the leader of the party called a halt and they sat down to eat some of the cassava and manioc cakes they had brought with them. The meal was washed down with a sour drink - something like buttermilk - contained in a huge earthen jar that one of the inferior tribe carried. They were in the midst of it when one of the hunters sprang to his feet with a guttural exclamation.

"Arjah!" he exclaimed and, though the boys did not understand his tongue, his attitude of alert attention signified that he said "Listen" as clearly as if he had used the word.

In an instant all of the party were on their feet and listening keenly. After a few seconds of strained attention the boys became aware of a sort of dull pounding sound which seemed to come from some distance. It sounded almost like the regular beat of a large drum. The air seemed to vibrate with it.

He leader of the party spoke a few words rapidly to the others and they all joined in a responsive shout which seemed to be one of assent to some proposition that had been made by him.

"He say elephant dance," said Umbashi; "him very dangerous when dance. He ask them they willing to go on. They all say yes."

Lathrop looked alarmed.

"Say, Billy," he whispered as they moved forward, "I don't mind a little danger, but going up against an elephant with a few tin spears looks to me like being little above the limit."

"Cheer up," replied the irrepressible reporter, "we've got to go on now. It would never do for us to show the white feather at this stage of the game. The tribe would regard us as miserable cowards and perhaps even put us to death."

So with faces that one at least of them had some difficulty to render' expressive of calm repose the two American boys marched along with the others. As they advanced the drumming grew louder and they could feel the earth shake as the ponderous beast that caused it went through his strange exercise.

The leader worked round till the party was advancing against the wind, as elephants have a keen scent, and had they traveled along down the wind he would have been sure to have taken alarm and dashed off only to return and do more damage later on. In this way the party was enabled to work up to within a few yards of the great beast without his having any warning of their approach. It was a strange sight they beheld as they stood on the edge of the little clearing where the great beast was going through his dance. With his trunk curled high above his great head the big pachyderm was solemnly twirling round and round in a sort of slow waltz and every time he brought a foot down it was with a crash that shook the forest about him. He was a ferocious looking brute, with a wicked gleam in his small eye that boded ill for anyone who should happen to get in his path. One of his tusks was broken off short, doubtless in some fight with another of his kind, and his body was plowed with scars and cuts - the relics of former battles. Altogether he was as wicked and menacing a looking brute as the boys had ever seen.

Suddenly he sighted the attacking party. The dance instantly stopped and he stood stock-still for an instant gazing at them while they promptly made for the trees and clambered up them by means of the lanyards of creepers that swung down from the tops.

Billy and Lathrop, however, were too much astonished by the sudden turn events had taken to follow the example of the savages and so stood gazing awestricken at the elephant while he gazed at them in apparent amazement at two boys having the temerity to face him in his native forest.

The situation was not to last long, however. Their guide, with the rest of the party, had hastily clambered into the trees and now he called to the boys loudly:

"Climb! climb!"

But the churns were too late.

As they turned to obey his instructions the great brute charged with a furious trumpet.

His first onslaught the boys avoided by slipping behind a tree, more from instinct than anything else. The impetus of the maddened animal's charge carried him by the tree and before he could stop himself and turn his ponderous body for a fresh attack he had gone some yards beyond the boys.

Bellowing with fury the huge creature made ready for fresh charge, but by this time Billy and Lathrop had seized the creepers and were both several feet above the ground. In his haste, however, Billy's luckless rifle twisted between his legs and almost caused a disaster. For a second he hung helpless, trying to kick the weapon free. But it hung by its leather shoulder band and he was unable to do so instantly.

The boy, with a despairing cry, gazed at the onrushing elephant and could almost feel himself being seized by its mighty trunk and dashed to death, when a pair of strong, black arms seized him and dragged him up to a place of safety. The man who had taken this risk was their friend Umbashi, and as Billy thanked him he felt a feeling of real respect for this half naked savage who had risked his life to save another's.

After two or three more charges the animal seemed to get tired of this method of attack and stood beneath the tree shaking with rage, very much like a bull that has driven a boy to refuge in an apple-tree. It was evident that it was time to either kill the brute or drive him off unless the party desired to spend an unlimited time in the trees.

"The fire-weapon," shouted Billy's friend, "use the fire-weapon."

Billy raised the long Arab weapon and fired. The bullet struck the elephant on the right ear with no more effect than to further anger him.

"Aim between the eyes," cried the savage.

Billy felt for a fresh cartridge and made a discovery.

In scrambling up the tree he had ripped off the skin bag

and his store of Arab cartridges, none too many, lay on the ground at the foot of the tree. When this intelligence was communicated to the tribesmen clinging in the other trees they held a shouted consultation the result of which was that, to the boys' amazement, one of them deliberately dropped to the ground and attracting the elephant's attention began to run him in circles. Now as the man could run fast and from time to time another took his place and the elephant had to use a lot of effort in turning corners, it soon became evident that the big pachyderm was tiring of the exercise.

It was evidently the intention of the natives to run him out and then spear him to death - but an unexpected happening put an end to this method of elephant hunting. One of the men who was worrying the great animal, much after the manner of a bull-fighter, suddenly caught his foot on a root and fell headlong. A shout went up as the others realized that he was doomed to almost certain death. Billy and Lathrop averted their eyes. It was terrible to have to sit there powerless and watch the sacrifice.

But even as they listened with sickened ears for the death-cry of the unfortunate victim and whilst the elephant's trumpet of triumph was still resounding, one of the flying men dropped, knife in hand, from his tree on to the monster's back.

He landed right behind the great creature's ears and as the animal threw back his trunk to whisk him off and annihilate him be plunged his weapon through the soft folds of skin at the base of the huge skull clear down into the brain.

It was a mortal wound.

As the elephant stopped short in his charge and began to stagger in his death throes the Flying Man slipped to the ground and picked up his comrade, who had swooned from terror.

Ten minutes later the great rogue elephant was beyond all further mischief and the boys joined as heartily as any of the others in congratulating the brave man whose unparalleled feat of heroism had saved his comrade's life.

The man's name was Aga, and the boys had reason later on to remember him for another deed which affected them even more nearly than the slaying of the elephant.

CHAPTER XVIII

A LINK FROM THE PAST

On their triumphal return to the cliff with the tusks of the slain elephant as trophies of the hunt a strange spectacle met the boys' eyes. Clustered about a sort of altar, which they had not noticed before, was a group of the cliff-dwellers who seemed to be deeply interested in something that was going forward. A loud sound of chanting and intoning of what seemed to be a solemn ritual was the first inkling the boys had of what was going on.

On joining the throng the lads found that it was some sort of a religious ceremony that was being proceeded with. A group of men in white flowing robes and high conical hats - decorated with mystic symbols worked out in precious stones that looked like rubies and emeralds, though of such size that this seemed scarcely credible - were walking round and round the altar in a sort of what the irreverent Billy termed "a cakewalk." Pausing at each corner and revolving slowly, three times they intoned the weird chant.

Suddenly the music took on a louder tone arid several men with clashing cymbals joined in. The auditors, too, fell flat on their faces and Billy and Lathrop, on the former's suggestion, did the same.

"Not to do as the others are doing might cost us our heads," sagely remarked the diplomatic Billy, "and I need mine in my business."

Whatever the nature of the ceremony, it was now evidently approaching a climax. The chanting grew louder and more furious and the cymbal players clashed their huge metal instruments together with a deafening clangor. Suddenly, from the passage from which the galleries branched off, there appeared six men clad in robes of flaming scarlet and conical caps of the same color.

They formed an escort to a pitiable figure.

That of a white bearded man who was bent with years and whose eyes gazed vacantly about him as he stumbled along between the red-robed dignitaries. But it was not his age and not his feebleness that made the boys' hearts beat quicker and caused a galvanic shock to shoot through them.

The man was white.

There was no doubt about it. In spite of his sun-browned skin and the barbarous ornaments that covered him, the figure in the center of the red-robed group was a Caucasian - perhaps an American - a fellow countryman.

And now the boys noticed with a shudder that in the hands of each of the red-robed men was a knife of some sort of stone - perhaps flint. These cruel looking weapons they brandished as they slowly paced forward in time to the chanting.

But their captive - if he were a captive seemed indifferent to all this. His dull eyes gazed straight ahead of him as if he were hypnotized - or, as was more probable, under the influence of some drug. As the group approached the altar the chanting suddenly stopped and the onlookers rose to their feet. From the altar now arose a thin spiral of smoke, the offspring of a fire kindled by one of the priests.

The sun was just setting and showed like a blood-red ball, through the mist that arose from low-lying garden lands. As its disk touched the horizon the chanting broke out afresh and the red-robed men seizing the old white man as if he were a beast dragged him forward and threw him on the altar.

And now for the first time came to the chums the horrifying realization of what the scene they were witnessing really meant.

The man was about to be sacrificed!

But even as the red-robed men raised their knives in unison and were about to give them the downward lunge that would extinguish the life of their feeble victim - and as the other priests and the audience turning toward the setting sun, chanted louder and more vociferously - a startling interruption occurred.

"By the holy poker you're not going to kill that old man while I can prevent it."

It was Billy Barnes; his face white and his lips set in a thin line of determination.

As he spoke utterly oblivious to the fact that not one of

the men could understand him - Lathrop, pale-faced also, stepped forward by his side.

And there stood the two American boys while the auditors - at first dumb with amazement - began to buzz angrily like a nest of disturbed hornets.

One of the white-robed priests gave a sharp order and once more the red-garbed executors raised their knives.

Billy quietly, though his heart was beating almost to suffocation, slipped a cartridge from the recovered bag into his Arab rifle. He leveled it at the red-robed knife wielders.

"The first man that moves I'll shoot!"

Although the words were as unintelligible to the priests and the cliff-dwellers as any that had gone before, the gesture with which Billy raised the rifle to his shoulder and covered the group was eloquent enough. And as it happened, the delay saved the old man's life; for while they hesitated the sun rushed below the horizon and the swift African night fell. A loud groan from the crowd announced that the hour for the culmination of the sacrifice had passed and that for the time being the intended victim's life was saved.

But for the boys the situation was serious enough. Powerless to resist such numbers they were seized by scores of the winged men and hustled into the passage, which was lit up by blazing torches of the same resinous wood that their guide had used on the first night that they came there. They were hurried along, their feet hardly touching the ground, till they reached one of the diverging galleries. Down this their captors shoved them till they reached a small cubical cell - windowless and without ventilation. Into this they were thrust and a huge stone door that hinged on some contrivance the boys could not understand swung to upon them with a dull bang. But a few minutes later it reopened and another prisoner was thrust in.

It was the aged captive whose life Billy had saved!

This much they saw in the momentary glare of the torches and then as the door closed the darkness - so black that you could feel it - shut down again. But Billy's reportorial curiosity, even in this situation, was still predominant.

"Who are you?" he asked eagerly of the new arrival, whose face he could not see and whose presence he could only guess at by the temporary revelation of the torch-light.

The only answer was a groan; but a few seconds later a voice that sounded strange from long disuse or unaccustomedness to the use of the English language replied:

"I have not heard a white man speak for forty years."

"What?" exclaimed the thunderstruck Billy.

"What I say is true and when you hear my name you will perhaps realize that fact. I am George Desmond the American explorer."

"The George Desmond who was lost in 1870?" cried Billy, almost choking with excitement.

"The same," was the reply in the same rusty voice, "like the sound of a long disused door swinging on its hinges," was the way Billy described it afterward in the article he wrote about the finding of George Desmond.

"But George Desmond was a man of thirty-five!" protested Billy, "when he was lost."

"And I am seventy-five," went on the sad voice in the blackness, "I was captured by the winged men in 1870. I have kept the record of the long years on a notched stick. I never expected to hear the sound of a fellow countryman's voice again."

The poor tired voice broke down, and in the darkness through which they could not see the boys heard the old man weeping.

"Great cats!" groaned Billy to Lathrop, whose hand he held so that they could be near together in the awful blackness, "forty years without seeing a white face - jumping horn-toads, what a fate!"

But the old man's soft weeping stopped presently and in a firmer voice he said:

"My wife and my sons? Can you tell me anything of them?"

As a newspaper man Billy recollected very clearly the space that had been given some five years before to the death, at a ripe old age, of the wife of George Desmond the lost explorer.

"She is dead," he said gently.

They heard the castaway sigh, and then he asked in a voice he strove to render firm, but which trembled in spite of itself:

"And my sons?"

"They are all alive and in business in New York," said Billy. "Your wife died believing to the end that you would come back. They placed her chair so that she could face the east. She died at daybreak with her eyes turned toward the sea beyond which lay Africa."

"Africa!" echoed the tired, disused voice. "Africa! it has cost me everything I had."

There was silence for some time after this. Neither of the boys wanted to intrude on the silent grief of the explorer so strangely found, though each was dying to ask him a host of questions. It was the aged man himself who broke the silence at length.

"But I am selfish," he exclaimed. "I should have thanked you before this for saving my life. The priests were determined that, as I was old and useless, my life should be offered to the Sun-god to appease a sickness that has of late carried off hundreds of the Flying Men. They are a dying race, young men. As a man of science, I predict that in five years or less there will not be a single one of the once numerous tribe alive. I have studied them closely and can predict their extinction."

"Then you have not been a prisoner always?" asked Billy.

"No, my young friend, I have not. When first I came here I was received warmly and was paid high honors.

I was allowed to record my observations in writing - fortunately I carried a supply of ink and paper."

"You still have the manuscript?" gasped Billy, with the reporter's instinct to the fore.

"I have," sighed old Mr. Desmond, "in the cell that I so long called home then, the pages still lie. But I have neglected them for many years. I had no more writing materials when I used up my slender supply and I never thought to regain civilization.

"But now did you ever get here?" asked the amazed Billy.

"That is a long story," replied the captive, "but briefly told, it is as follows: In the season of 1870, as you perhaps know, my ill-fated expedition left Grand Bassam. My avowed object was to collect specimens and data for the Smithsonian Institute, but my real and secret desire was to find the tribe of Flying Men of whose existence I had heard in a fragmentary way on previous expeditions to the West Coast. I have found them - " he went on with a heavy sigh - "but at what a cost - at what a cost!"

There was silence for a few minutes and then the old voice went on, gaining in strength as he proceeded, and resumed acquaintance with words to which his tongue had been long unused.

"My expedition, as you know, was never heard of again. The reason was this. In some way the Arab slave-traders - who were thick in this district then and plied their nefarious trade almost openly - gained the belief that my expedition was a pretense for a plan of espionage on them and they attacked my camp one night and slaughtered every man in it but myself. Why they did not kill me I do not know, unless it was because of the intercession of a young Arab, a mere youth and the son of the chief. I have never forgotten his name or his kindness."

"What was his name?" asked Billy, who was deeply interested and wanted to get every detail of the extraordinary story.

"Muley-Hassan!" was the amazing reply.

"Muley-Hassan," echoed Billy, "why, he is the most cold-blooded fiend in the slave-trade to-day."

"Perhaps," answered the old man, "but he was good to me when he was a young man and I have never forgotten it."

"Well," he went on, picking up his narrative, "it was not long before retribution overtook the Arabs. One night their camp was attacked by a tribe whose village they had raided and sacked some time before and only a few of them escaped, among them must have been Muley-Hassan, though, till you told me of him, I believed him dead. The savages, seeing that I was not one of the Arab race took care of me and I fared well at their hands. But a great longing to see civilization - to clasp my wife in my arms, to see my children and America once more, was always with me, and one night I escaped from their village. I wandered half-delirious from fever and starvation for many days after that, for I lost my way in the forest, and, as I had no compass, wandered aimlessly seeking a river by which I might follow down to the coast. One night such a sharp attack of fever overtook me that I was-stricken unconscious. I gave myself up for dead before I lost my senses and only recollect awaking in this village. From that day to this, although I have repeatedly endeavored to escape I have never been able to do so. The ladder is guarded day and night," - (this information dashed a half-formed hope in Billy's mind of escape by that way,) "and it would be suicide to attempt to penetrate the great jungles on the other side. I thought to end my days here, but I never dreamed till the other day that my life was destined to end as it would have, had it not been for your brave intervention.

"The malady of which I have spoken has devastated almost every family in the cliff and at the instigation of Agagi, the head priest - a man who has always hated my influence over his people - I was blamed by the other priests for being the cause of the affliction.

"They pretended to have a revelation from the Sun-god stating that if my life were sacrificed the curse that rested on the cliff-dwellers would be removed. Accordingly I was seized and chained and would certainly have died had it not been for you. But alas, young men, I fear you are doomed to forfeit your lives as the cost of rescuing an old man who is not long for this life in any event. I wish that you had been far away and had never had the brave impulse to risk your young lives for my worthless old one."

Now it is a remarkable thing, but Billy, who should have replied to the aged man in all sorts of high-sounding language, could find nothing to reply to this but:

Oh, that's all right."

"I think you are the bravest boys I have ever heard of," the old man was beginning when a soft "hiss-s-st!" caused them all to turn their eyes to the direction in which they knew the door lay, and from which the sound had proceeded.

"H-s-s-s-t," came the sound again.

Did it mean a friend or an enemy?

CHAPTER XIX

FRIENDS IN NEED

They were not kept long in suspense. After being assured that their attention was attracted, the voice that had made the hissing signal whispered through some aperture of which the boys had no knowledge:

"Listen to me, white boys, and you, too, old man, you can escape if your hearts are stout."

Stunned by the suddenness of this joyful news the boys sat silent.

"Are you listening, white boys?" said the voice impatiently.

"Yes - yes," whispered Billy eagerly.

"Then when a man comes in a short time to you with food and drink do not touch it, for it is poisoned with a deadly drug; but curb your appetite. In a short time the same man will come back to see if you have yet become insensible. Then you must be of stout heart and leap upon him and kill him. After that leave your cell and I will show you how to gain freedom."

The boys had recognized the voice at once as that of

their friendly guide, though why he should have taken such a risk to aid them did not manifest itself till he whispered:

"And as a reward, I ask of the fat white boy with the glass eyes his fire-weapon which assuredly contains a great fetish and of the red-headed one some of his hair for a fetish also. Of the old man I would have the round box containing the strange god that says by day and by night 'tick-tick'."

"He means my watch," answered the old man, "it was a present from my dead wife to me on our wedding day, but he shall have it."

The boys also promised their "fetishes."

There was a guttural sound of satisfaction from outside the cell as the bargain was struck and then all was silent.

How they passed the time till the door swung open and the man whom their friend had foretold would bring them food and drink appeared, they never knew; but somehow it went. The new comer set the stuff down without a word and then stuck the flaming torch he carried in a niche in the wall so that they might have light to eat by. He made several gesticulations intended, apparently, to signify that what he had set before them was very good.

"Hum," said Billy when he had gone, "I'd as soon eat a mess of toads as touch any of this stuff - although it smells mighty good," he added regretfully, "and I'm hungry enough to gobble up a crocodile, claws and all."

But they all abstained from touching it and spent the time between the second promised visit discussing whether they would carry out the instructions of the friendly savage.

"But we can't kill the fellow," objected Lathrop.

"Certainly not," replied Billy; "but, now that we have a light, I see that there is a nice convenient chain fastened to the wall over there. There would be no objection to our gagging him, to prevent any outcry, and then hitching him up with it."

"But he is a pretty husky-looking customer," objected Lathrop; "suppose we can't overcome him?"

"We'll have to take our chances on that," said Billy decisively. "Now what I propose is, that when he comes back we all he stretched out as if the drug had overcome us and then, when I give the word, we all jump on him."

He looked doubtfully at the old man as he spoke. There was no question that in such a struggle the explorer would be worse than useless. Mr. Desmond himself agreed with Billy and it was arranged that while the two boys grappled with the negro that the old man should pull the door to - in the event of its being left open - so that no noise of the struggle might penetrate into the passage outside.

The little party immediately spread themselves out on the floor in well simulated insensibility and waited with hearts that beat uncomfortably quick for the decisive moment to arrive.

Failure meant death but, as Billy had put it, they were due to die anyhow it seemed and they owed it to themselves to make as brave an effort as possible to escape such a fate.

At last they heard a fumbling at the door and the man who had brought them the drugged food entered the cell. He scrutinized them with a grunt of satisfaction and going up to each one shook him by the shoulder to see if they were only asleep or really insensible. Apparently he was satisfied from their inertness that the drug had worked, for he muttered to himself rapidly in the unknown tongue as he concluded his examination.

Then he turned to pick up the earthen dishes, stooping over with his back to Billy Barnes as he did so.

It was Billy's move!

Like a flash the young reporter - who had earned an enviable record on the gridiron and crew at Columbia University - was on the savage's back while Lathrop rushed at the fellow as he straightened up and gave him a low tackle. As Billy leaped he had dug his fingers into the fellow's windpipe to choke any outcry, and when Lathrop seized him by the legs he toppled over like a felled ox without uttering a sound. Billy rolled from under him as he fell backward and the man's head struck the stone floor with a terrific crash.

He was knocked insensible by the fall. The moment to escape had arrived!

Rapidly the boys tore a strip off Billy's shirt and formed it into a gag. With other strips they tied the insensible man's hands behind his back and manacled his legs.

"He won't come to for quite a while after the crack he got," remarked Billy; "but in case he does, he won't be able to attract attention for a long time."

Then, as cautiously as though stepping on eggs, they tiptoed out into the passage - after extinguishing the torch - and the next minute were startled to be suddenly halted by a form that ran right into them in the blackness.

The next minute, however, their anxiety was relieved. It was Umbashi who had collided with them and accompanying him was Aga, the man who killed the rogue elephant. It appeared that the two had agreed to divide the fetishes their captives were to give them in return for their freedom. And Aga at once, with a stone knife, cut off two generous locks of Lathrop's hair.

"But how are you to get my gun," objected Billy, "the priests took it from me?"

"I already have it, Boy-of-the-eyes-of-glass," replied the engaging cliff-dweller. "I stole it from the old head-priest while he slept. But you must give it me of your own free will, or it will not be good 'fetish.'"

Of course Billy willingly "gave."

To get the watch they had to traverse what seemed to Billy and Lathrop in their feverish excitement miles and miles of passages. But apparently the cliff-dwellers all went to bed early and slept sound for they encountered no one, and their guides did not seem to be in any anxiety over the possibility of discovery. Once they got a chill of horror when just before they left the cell door Aga, who carried a sharp knife - the same with which he had dispatched the elephant and cut Lathrop's hair - signified his intention of cutting the unconscious meal-bringer's throat. It was with great difficulty that the boys dissuaded him from this barbaric act, the horror of which did not seem to appeal either to him or his savage companion.

Once in old Desmond's cell it did not take long to get the watch - an aged gold key-winder - and present it to the delighted savages. But several precious minutes were lost in showing the two how to wind it up. They regarded the key with quite as much veneration as the watch. The boys saw the old man's eyes filled with tears as he handed it over and Billy, as he saw the inscription on it, in a quaint, old-fashioned script, realized why.

"To my dear husband, George Desmond, on our wedding day, May 24th 1874;" it read. With the signature "Mary Desmond."

Before they left the place that had been his home for the majority of his long life, the old man carefully drew from beneath the palm fiber covering of the niche that served him as a bed a pile of yellowed paper, covered closely with fine writing in a clear, bold hand. The pages had been written many years before old age had seized their author's hand and paralyzed his strength.

Billy realized with a thrill that these papers contained, the imperishable record of the long-lost scientist's observations and commentaries on the mysterious

Flying Men.

But it was no time to linger in speculations.

Hastily thrusting the papers into the bosom of his shirt the aged man signified to his guides that he was, ready, and they left the chamber that had housed him for so many years - without regret on his part you may be sure.

Silently as cats they slipped down the corridor and, after about a quarter of an hour of traversing its smooth floor, they found themselves at the hole which gave egress to the outside world and from which hung the rope-ladder by which they were to descend to freedom.

Aga and the other savage gave grunts of pleasure and even laughed softly as the boys' with a horrified start, almost stumbled over a recumbent figure.

It was that of the guard of the ladder.

He lay as if dead - his body right across the narrow entrance. The moonlight from the outside that flooded the entrance showed that his mouth was open and his eyes closed.

A sudden rage filled Billy as he looked on the victim of what seemed to him to have been a wanton murder.

"You have killed him," he said raising his voice imprudently in his anger.

"Hush, boy-with-the-glass-eyes," exclaimed Urnbashi, "he is not dead. In a few hours he will be as well as you or I, but he will recollect nothing. We have given him the sleeping root that brings oblivion."

And now it was time to take the final step.

"A canoe with food and a jar of water is at the foot of the ladder," whispered their guide, "and the current will carry you down toward the coast. It will not be a hard journey except for the Tunnel of the Roaring Waters. Only a few men have navigated that and escaped alive, but you will be compelled to traverse it to reach the coast."

"Can we not leave the canoe and go overland round the tunnel?" asked Billy rightly conjecturing that their guide referred to a place where the river ran underground when he spoke of the Tunnel of the Roaring Waters.

"That cannot be done," was the African's reply. "The swamps where the sleeping death (the sleeping sickness) lies are all about it. Only by way of the Tunnel of the Roaring Waters can you escape."

"There is one other way," began Aga, "but that lies through the forest."

"We will take it rather than risk navigation in such a torrent as you describe," decided Billy after the remark of Aga had been translated to him.

But before the two savages could say more there came a distant booming borne down the rocky tube of the corridor.

It was the far-off confused sound of excited voices.

"Quick! glass-eyes, your escape has been discovered; you haven't a moment to lose!" cried Umbashi.

It was only too evident that he spoke the truth. The roar of the searchers' angry voices was rapidly ringing louder.

"Take this, white boys, and defend yourselves to the death rather than be recaptured," said their friend as he thrust a stone knife into Billy's hand.

The old man and Lathrop were already half-away down the swaying ladder.

"Be careful, for the river is swollen with the melting snows of the mountains and runs as if a million demons were in its soul to-night," warned Unbashi.

With a quick "Good-bye" to the men who risked their lives to rescue them, Billy took his place on the swinging ladder and followed the others down.

They were not a second too soon.

Even as they took their places in the canoe and Billy prepared to slash the grass-rope that held it, the clamor drew close to the mouth of the tunnel.

From the foot of the cliff the chums and their aged companion saw torches glowing and could perceive Aga and the other pointing at them and evidently explaining to the tribesmen that they had tried to stop their flight. Billy was glad to see that apparently their explanations were accepted and they were not suspected of having aided the escaping prisoners.

With a quick slash of his flint knife, the young reporter severed the rope at which the canoe was straining till it was taut as a piano wire. There were several other canoes lying alongside and before he cast loose Billy cut the detaining ropes of these also.

"Now they'll have to swim if they want to get us!" he exclaimed as the canoe, released from its bondage, shot forward on the boiling current at a dizzy rate.

But he had reckoned without the flying men. Dozens of them had dropped from their holes and having gained the opposite bank started in pursuit of the boys and the old explorer, who lay as if overcome at the bottom of the canoe. Many of the strange beings carried bows and arrows and they sent their shafts whizzing in a shower at the canoe. One pierced its side and Billy had to stop the hole with a strip torn from his already ripped-up shirt.

But fortunately, except for a slight scratch on Billy's forearm, none of the arrows did much harm to the voyagers themselves, and borne on the swift current the canoe soon outdistanced her pursuers.

As the sound of their shouting grew faint behind them, Billy and Lathrop grasped the paddle with which they strove to keep the boat on a straight course - there was no need to propel her.

The young reporter realized that three lives - his own, Lathrop's and that of the long missing explorer depended alone now on their skill and grit.

CHAPTER XX

THE SMOKE READER

And now we must leave the floating canoe with its occupants and turn to the River Camp, where we left the Boy Aviators overcome with anxiety as to the fate of their young comrades. The situation was indeed one calculated to try the stoutest heart. There was only one drop of sweet in their cup of bitter.

Harry, poking about among the ruins of the deserted camp, had discovered several cans of gasoline that the raiders had overlooked. They formed sufficient fuel with the picric cakes that Frank still had a supply of, to drive the big aeroplane for several hundred miles if the wind conditions were favorable.

But leave the river camp the boys dare not, for they realized that if Billy and Lathrop did manage to make their escape, they would, if possible, come back there. True, it was a chance so remote as to appear almost impossible, but under the circumstances even the shadow of a hope seemed to assume substance. And so they waited, and had been waiting, while the stirring events we have related had been happening to their missing chums.

As if to add to their oppression, old Sikaso mooned

about the camp, his eyes rooted to the ground in moody absorption and muttering to himself, "five go - three come back," till Frank angrily ordered him to stop. The realization that his gloomy prophecy seemed only too likely to be fulfilled, however, did not tend to relieve the situation.

"If we do not hear from them to-morrow, we shall be compelled to take to the air and fly to the coast," said Frank as they sat that evening round a camp-fire which had been lighted to keep away marauding lions, whose roars ever and anon shook the forest. At such times old Sikaso's eyes wandered longingly to his great war-axe. There is little doubt that he would have liked to work off his gloomy feelings by tackling a lion single-handed with his weapon.

"You think, then, it isn't worth while waiting if we have heard no news by then?" asked Harry.

"It isn't that," said Frank in reply, "but we have not provisions left to more than tide us over another day. What the Arabs didn't destroy they spoiled."

Harry nodded his head silently.

Cruel necessity, it seemed, was to compel them to evacuate the camp, to which they still clung in the hope the lost adventurers might return.

It was in vain Ben Stubbs cracked his jokes that night and related all sorts of droll sea yarns in the hope of cheering up his young companions. For the first time since he had known them it looked as if the Boy Aviators had really lost all hope, and truly the facts seemed to warrant the stoutest-heart in the world being downcast - to say the least.

Suddenly without a word old Sikaso left the fire and strode off into the forest. He was gone for more than an hour and when he came back his look of gloom had vanished. For him he was almost cheerful.

He swung his terrible axe in all sorts of fantastic evolutions and hummed to himself his grim chant with a fierce sort of joy.

"White boys, the smoke is going to tell me things to-night," he exclaimed suddenly. "When the moon reaches to the top of the sky I shall tell you news of the four-eyed one and of the red-headed."

Impatiently they waited till the moon reached her zenith and then watched wonderingly while the old savage built a small fire of sticks, over each one of which he mumbled something in African.

"What good does he suppose all this hocus-pocus is going to do us?" muttered Harry irritably, "as if an old fire could tell us anything we didn't know already. It's all rubbish, I say."

"I'm not so sure," remarked Frank thoughtfully. "We have already seen something of what his skill can do and I don't mind letting him see if he can't conjure up something to give us a ray of hope."

"Oh bosh, Frank," replied Harry, "if he ever did get anything right through this rigmarole and hanky-panky it was simply because he had good luck. That's all."

"For my part, I've knocked around the world too much

to be so cock sure of some things as some young chaps seem to be," put in Ben Stubbs, with a chuckle, looking up from the frying-pan that he was scouring with sand.

Harry looked abashed and said nothing.

If old Sikaso had heard any of this colloquy he made no sign, but with the face of a graven image went about his preparations. Slowly he struck the sparks from his never-failing flint and steel, and a few seconds later the little fire was sending up a blaze.

"Do you see anything?" asked Frank.

"Too soon now, wait till smoke come," he said, and resumed his intense watching of the fire.

After a delay that seemed maddening, to two at least of the group that was watching, the old Krooman announced that all was ready.

Even Harry felt a thrill of interest as the old man began to spin slowly on his toes round the column of smoke, chanting slowly some strange mixture of savage music which was, as Frank guessed, an incantation to the fetish that, as he believed, dwelt in the smoke. As the smoke grew thicker he cast some sort of powder from a skin-bag into it and instantly a thick yellow column of vapor shot up.

The whole forest about seemed impregnated with the strong odor of the stuff and the boys' eyes smarted. Old Sikaso kept up his dance, bending lower and lower till it seemed that he must be actually inhaling the pungent, acrid smoke.

As this strange scene progressed, Frank felt his eyes begin to grow dim and an unaccountable languor fill his limbs. His head swam round and he desired nothing so much as to lie down and sleep -- and yet a compelling power forced him to keep his eyes fixed on the column of smoke over which the aged Krooman was now stooping with outspread hands.

Suddenly he gave a sharp cry - an exclamation almost of command.

"Look - look, white boys, and you, old man of the sea and the forests of the far-off land, and I shall show you the magic of the sleeping heart of Africa."

With eyes that started from his head Frank gazed, in obedience to a majestic sweep of the African's hand, full into the ascending column of yellowish smoke.

The languor the boy had felt at first had now quite left him and he was only intent on seeing what was about to transpire.

Sikaso's voice once more rose in his dismal chant and he cast more of the powder from his skin-bag into the fire. The smoke pillar grew to an immense size and, as he gazed at it, before Frank's amazed eyes a scene as strange to him as any he had ever set eyes on, began slowly to take shape.

There was a river edge with mighty banks at the summit of which waved fronds of tropical plants and in which huge beasts, that he recognized as hippopotami, wallowed and sputtered. An unhealthy steam arose from the banks and the river boiled angrily along between its confines in a dark mud-colored flood.

So far the scene was not unlike the river in which he and Harry had so nearly lost their lives, but as he gazed the details grew clearer, as if it had been a magic lantern view, growing by degrees stronger and every outline of the tropical view was suddenly thrown into strong relief.

All at once the boy uttered a sharp cry, which was echoed by his brother and Ben. Old Sikaso never moved a muscle but kept on chanting.

Into the center of the wonderful smoke picture there had swum a canoe.

And in it were seated Billy Barnes and Lathrop!

With them, too, was the figure of a venerable white bearded man who seemed to be about to collapse. From time to time he raised himself feebly and gazed ahead. Frank could see Billy at such times stoop forward and speak to him.

The boys' plight was evidently a terrible one.

Their clothes were ripped and torn and Billy's shirt scarcely covered his body; which was a mass of cuts and scratches. A great cloud of mosquitoes hung about the canoe, clearly maddening its occupants with their myriads of tiny stings. The faces of both the young navigators were drawn and lined with anxiety as they paddled ahead in the turbulent current.

"See," cried Sikaso harshly, as the picture faded, "do the white boys still doubt?"

"No, no!" cried Harry. "Show us more, Sikaso."

The Krooman cast more of the magic powder into the dying fire and again a thick pillar of smoke curled upward.

His low crooning chant then began once more.

As before the picture did not assume shape at once but swam, as it were, slowly into view. This time the surroundings had changed. There was a look of agonized terror on the faces of all the occupants of the canoe as she seemed to be literally hurled forward upon a current that ran as swiftly as a mill race.

The frail craft rocked terribly and once or twice she shipped some water that Lathrop instantly bailed out with a shallow earthen dish.

Frank could almost hear the roar of the water as he gazed in silent fascination on the mysterious pictures of the smoke.

And now the apprehension on the faces of the occupants of the canoe was agonizing to watch. Once Frank saw the old man arise as if to cast himself into the water rather than face what lay ahead, but Lathrop instantly drew him back.

Again the picture died out and again the old Krooman. threw on more powder. As the smoke rolled up once more no one spoke. The situation was far too tense for that.

The scene now seemed to show that indeed all was over with the occupants of the canoe. The frail craft was seen to be in a tunnel of rough stone through which the roaring vortex of the waters poured with such violence that the boys and their aged companion were continually drenched with spray. Lathrop had hard work to keep the craft free of water now, and bailed incessantly. The old man was on his knees his hands clasped and his lips moving as if in prayer. Billy, his face set, sat in the stern. Again and again with a quick twist of his paddle he saved the canoe from annihilation in the boiling current.

It was an agonizing scene to watch, and to the onlookers it seemed as real as if they had been gazing at the peril itself instead of its counterfeit presentment in smoke-pictures.

At last the walls of the tunnel were seen to widen out and the current to move more slowly. Frank gave a sigh of relief which was echoed by the others as the canoe emerged from the subterranean river into a broad lagoon with low banks covered with tropical verdure and seemingly, from the absence of steaming vapors a healthy spot. But even as the canoe entered the quiet waters a great body projected itself through the water followed by three other bulky forms.

They were recognized instantly by the watchers as hippopotami.

The leader of the animals made straight for the canoe, and the watchers trembled as they looked, for it was evident that one snap of the creatures' huge jaws would cave in the side of the canoe as if it were an eggshell.

With trembling excitement the Boy Aviators saw their young companions with both paddles make desperately for the shore, but before they reached it one of the hippopotami intercepted them, and with a charge of angry fury literally tossed the boat clean out of the water.

A second later the gazers at the smoke pictures saw the two missing adventurers and their aged unknown companion struggling in the water. It seemed that all was over when a strange interruption occurred.

A long, dark horny head with two cruel eyes and rows of saw-like teeth in its long jaws, sped through the waters. The hippopotamus turned savagely on the intruder and the two snapped savagely at each other for several minutes when the crocodile, mortally wounded to judge by the red swirl on the surface of the stream, made off.

But Billy and Lathrop were seen to have taken advantage of the brief breathing spell it gave them. In a few strong strokes they had swum with the aged man to shallow water and quickly waded ashore. They were safe then for the time being. But for how long?

Frank saw the two comrades gaze about them in despair at the wilderness of jungle that closed about them on every side. He saw them cast horrified looks at each other at the situation in which they found themselves - lost in the trackless African forests.

The next minute the old man fell forward on his face and lay still. Whether he was dead or unconscious, Frank could not, of course, tell - and then the smoke died out, and the picture faded.

CHAPTER XXI

THE CHUMS RESCUED BY AEROPLANE

Hope had almost died in the boys' hearts at the scene they had witnessed by means of powers that seemed incredible to them, but which several well known travelers have told us are not uncommon among certain natives of West Africa. But old Sikaso was destined to raise their hopes.

"We will save Four-Eyes and the Red-Headed one," he exclaimed suddenly.

"But how?" chorused the amazed three.

"In the ship that like the bird can cleave the air we will fly to them," was the astonishing reply.

"But we do not know where they are," objected Harry.

"I do," was the quiet response.

"What?"

"Say that again!"

"Well, I'll be hornswoggled!"

These exclamations came from each of the three in turn.

"They are on the banks of a river which I know well. In the smoke I recognized it. Few men have ever navigated the Tunnel of Death and came out to tell the tale, but your great white Fetish must have looked after them."

"You know the river?"

"Well do I know it white boy," replied the Krooman. "In the days when my limbs were supple I have hunted and fished there with others of my tribe."

"You can guide us to it?"

"I can."

"When?"

"As soon as it is dawn."

"How far is it from here?"

"Not more than a hundred and fifty miles."

Frank held up a moistened finger. The air was as calm as a mill-pond.

"We can make that distance in a little more than four hours," he announced.

It was Sikaso's turn to be astonished.

"Of a truth the magic of the white man is not as the

magic of the black man, but it is good," he said; "yes, it is good. In four hours. That is indeed mighty magic."

"Who can the old man be whom we saw with them?" asked Harry eagerly, his mind no longer containing an ounce of skepticism to the marvels he had seen.

"I have no idea," rejoined Frank, "but he was white evidently."

"I've seen his picture some place, sometime - or some chap that looked a powerful sight like him, only younger," said Ben, who doubtless had a vague recoll- ection of the once widely distributed photographs of the missing explorer Desmond.

"I am afraid that he was seriously ill, or even dying, from the last glimpse we had of him," said Frank gravely.

"Why could you not show us more smoke pictures Sikaso?" asked Harry eagerly.

"I have no more of the powder left," replied the old Krooman bending over his beloved axe and feeling the edge with a critical thumb. "Moreover, the smoke does not reveal the future."

There was, naturally enough, no thought of sleep that night, and so excited were the boys that they did not even feel the want of it. A huge shallow pit was dug back in the forest and the ivory taken from the chassis of the aeroplane and the aerial express wagon cached there and leaves and grass strewn over the place to make it as inconspicuous as possible. This was done before the aeroplane was got in readiness for the dash to the rescue.

"For," said Frank, "old Muley-Hassan, when he finds we have overreached him, may take a fancy to come back and try to wipe us out."

"Muley-Hassan will not fight with the few men he has left," sagely remarked old Sikaso; "when he has many he is brave as a lion, but when his followers are few he fights like the fox with wits against wits and few are his match for cunning."

As the day-life of the jungle - which has a nightlife as well as a daylight one - as the day-life of the forest began with the first ghostly gray of the dawn the boys swallowed a hasty meal, though they were almost too excited to eat in spite of Ben Stubbs' insistence that they take some nourishment. At the old sailor's suggestion, too, the car of the Golden Eagle II was packed with food for the castaways, who surely, from the latest glimpse they had had of them, must be in dire straits.

These preparations completed, they clambered into the car of the air-ship and with Frank at the wheel and the old Krooman at his elbow to direct the course they were to take, they left the ground and were soon flying through a breathless environment at sixty miles an hour.

The Golden Eagle II was on her way to the rescue.

"It is the end."

These words came from the feeble lips of Mr. Desmond as he lay beneath a rough screen of leaves and branches which the boys had erected to keep the heat of the African day from the dying man - for that he was dying they sadly realized.

The excitement of their flight and the peril of the subterranean river had been too much for the enfeebled frame and George Desmond's troubled soul was on its way to more peaceful rest than he had known in many years.

"Is there nothing we can do for you, sir?" asked Billy eagerly, bending over the dying man and taking his hand-which, despite the heat, was as cold as ice, between his.

"Nothing," whispered Desmond faintly, and then, with a supreme effort, he spoke once more.

"My papers - the history of the Flying Men."

He feebly indicated that he wished Billy to take them from his shirt.

The young reporter swiftly drew out the yellowed manuscript and reverently laid it before the fast-fading eyes. A faint smile overspread the aged man's careworn face.

"I commend them to your care," he said, as though every word now cost him an effort. "You have told me you are a newspaper reporter - you will see that they are given to the world?"

Billy once more taking the fast passing man's hand promised to fulfill this sacred trust.

"Read me the dedication," was the next whispered request of George Desmond.

In a trembling voice Billy read the words inscribed on the first page of the yellowed manuscript.

"To my dear wife Mary this volume is dedicated by her affectionate husband the Author."

"I never thought when I wrote those words I should die like this," exclaimed the dying man, "but it was to be. I always hoped that some day I would escape; but now that I have won freedom, rest seems to mean more to me than all else beside."

The tears welled into the eyes of both boys as with a resigned sigh George Desmond composed himself as if to sleep.

It was about five minutes later, and Billy still held the old man's hand, when the long-lost explorer raised himself on his elbow and shading his eyes with his trembling hand gazed in front of him as if he saw a vision.

"Mary - " he cried in a loud voice and fell back dead.

And so died George Desmond, the famous African traveler, almost within sight of the civilization to which he had so long dreamed of returning.

The shocked and grieved boys had hardly recovered their composure after this tragic termination of a brave man's life when Lathrop, who had been gazing despairingly about him gave a great shout.

The next minute it was echoed by Billy.

Half mad with joy the boys embraced each other and shook hands till it seemed they would fall off, and performed a dozen mad antics.

For, winging its way steadily toward them, though still at a great distance, was an aeroplane that they had no difficulty in recognizing at once as the Golden Eagle II.

There is no need to detail the scene that ensued when, fifteen minutes later, the great air-craft settled down on the river bank and the ravenous boys - who had long since exhausted the provisions in the boat - had been fed, and plied with questions till they had to stop eating to talk and stop talking to eat, at short intervals.

To the great joy of old Sikaso, who regarded it as a personal vindication of his powers, every detail of the trip through the subterranean river and the subsequent peril into which they had fallen was substantiated by Billy and Lathrop as having occurred exactly as it did in the smoke pictures. But there was a note of sadness amid all their joy in the death of the old explorer. On the river bank they dug a grave and marked it with a pile of rocks and there the remains of George Desmond rest for all time in the country to whose exploration he gave his life.

The Golden Eagle II had to make two trips between the river camp and the outlet of the subterranean river as, stout craft though she was, her gasoline supply was getting so low that Frank did not dare to run her at top speed and consequently she would not carry more than three passengers. By nightfall, however, the reunited adventurers were all seated about their campfire and talking and retelling all that had happened to each other during their separation.

Their conversation was interrupted by a strange happening.

The puff-puff of the steam launch that had brought them tip the river was suddenly heard and as she drew alongside the steep bank a familiar figure stepped from her side into the bright moonlight.

Not one of the party that did not give a start of amazed surprise as in the newcomer they recognized:

Luther Barr, of New York!

CHAPTER XXII

LUTHER BARR'S TRICK

The astonishing meeting in the remote wilds of the African forest with a man they instinctively mistrusted bereft the lads of words for an interval.

Frank was the first to find his voice:

"Why, Mr. Barr, what are you doing here?" he exclaimed amazedly.

But if the boys seemed astonished Mr. Barr retained his usual icicle-like attitude. Except that he was dressed in tropical white and wore a huge pith helmet which set above his ill-favored features "like a mushroom over a toad," as Billy described it later, he might have just stepped out of his office on Wall Street, instead of from a wheezy launch on a steaming subequatorial river.

"Good-evening, boys, a little late for dinner, I see, but I daresay you can cook me something. After dinner I want to talk to you. I have come a long way for the purpose so you can guess my business is of importance."

"Of importance ? I should say so;" sputtered the

irrepressible Billy. "Pray did you come by air-ship, Mr. Barr?"

"No, sir, I came in my yacht the Brigand. She is almost as fast as a liner and as I came direct to this port I didn't take more than half the time occupied by you boys on the voyage."

"You had a good trip?" asked Frank as Mr. Barr sat down and began eating the hastily prepared meal which Ben served him.

"Yes, splendid;" said Mr. Barr, "we had one misfortune though. When we were two days out my captain - a splendid man, boys - slipped on the wet foredeck as the yacht was plowing through a heavy sea and struck on his head on a stanchion."

"I hope he was not badly hurt," said Frank.

"He is dead," said Mr. Barr, calmly stuffing half a sweet potato into his capacious mouth.

The boys gave an exclamation of concern.

"Yes, it was very annoying," commented Mr. Barr.

"You see I have had to trust since to the navigation of my mate, and while he is a careful fellow he is not much good as a navigator, and in addition to that he is a drinking man. I am afraid that he may be ashore now in my absence and indulging his taste for strong drink."

"I should have thought you would have forbidden him shore leave," commented Harry.

"No good, my dear boy, that fellow would swim ashore even if the harbor were swarming with sharks, to gratify his disgusting taste."

"But now," he continued with a change of tone, "to business. You have got the ivory?

"We have," replied Frank.

"Where?"

"We have it here," was the quiet rejoinder.

"What!" an amazed tone.

"What I tell you is true," and Frank-foolishly as he admitted afterward-led the way to the cache in the forest; "it is buried here so as to be safe from marauders."

Mr. Barr seemed lost in thought for a few minutes then he suggested a return to the camp-fire. Once there he drew out a paper from his pocket-book.

"Many things have happened since you left New York, boys," he said quietly, through a feverish gleam in his deep, crafty eyes belied his outward calm.

"This paper," he continued, holding it out, "is signed by Mr. Beasley, it resigns to me all claim in the ivory and I am here to take it.'"

"Let me look at that paper."

It was Lathrop who spoke.

The boy's cheeks were angrily flushed and his eyes bad a dangerous flash.

"That is not my father's signature!"

"What do you mean?"

"Exactly what I say - that this writing which purports to be my father's was never penned by him."

"You are making a rash assertion."

"I am fully prepared to prove it when we get back to New York."

"And in the meantime the Boy Aviators retain their claim on the ivory that we fought so hard to get," put in Frank.

Old Mr. Barr turned on him with a wolfish fury.

Indeed in his rage he resembled nothing so much as a long, lean, timber wolf deprived of his expected prey.

"We will see all about that!" he raged. "There is a law in Fort Assini though there may not be here. I have this paper here which in the eyes of the law is a legal transfer to me of Beasley's claim on the ivory. It is mine now and I mean to have it."

Frank's heart sank. He did not know much about law and it looked as if old man Barr held the upper hand.

"But that is not my father's signature or writing," cried Lathrop.

"That will be a matter for the American courts to decide," was the frigid reply.

"I shall lay the whole matter before M. Desplaines - the consular agent of our government," cried Frank at last.

"It is too late to do that," retorted Mr. Barr, "anticipating that there would be some trouble I have already engaged a lawyer and M. Desplaines will keep his hands off this affair."

"Why did you anticipate trouble?" shot out Frank, "was it because you knew that signature was false?"

For a fragment of a second the old man's pale face grew paler - or rather turned a sickly yellow.

"Bah," he said the next minute, "this is a business matter and not one for boys to enter into. I will see that you are well paid for your part of the work. If you like I will write you a check now."

He drew out an ever-ready check-book and fountain pen.

"I would rather have fair play than money," was Frank's stinging retort.

"And so say we all of us," chorused Harry, Billy and Lathrop.

Mr. Barr was plainly irritated. In a snappish tone he said at length:

"If you can show me where I am to sleep I think I will

go to bed. I am very tired. We will discuss this matter further to-morrow."

Ben Stubbs, with a very ill grace, made up a bed for the New Yorker at some distance from the others.

"I'd like to stuff it full of barb-wire," he confided to Frank afterward.

As for Sikaso, he eyed old Mr. Barr from time to time, and then eyed his axe in a way that made it very plain that the two were connected in his mind in a manner that would have made it very uncomfortable for the old financier.

But if Mr. Barr felt the atmosphere of repugnance to him that pervaded the camp he did not show it.

He rolled up in his blanket as if he had been used to a rough bed all his life and was soon apparently wrapped in deep sleep. The boys, tired out as they were and not a little downcast at the turn events had taken, soon followed him. An hour later the River Camp was as silent as a graveyard with the exception of Ben Stubbs' mighty snores.

It was then that old Mr. Barr, who had seemed so sound asleep, cautiously raised his head from his blankets and peered about him.

After a few minutes of this he slipped into the few clothes he had discarded when he went to bed and tiptoed past the sleeping adventurers down to the river bank and the launch.

There was an evil smile on his face as he went that to

those who knew Luther Barr would have said as plain as print "Some mischief is in the wind."

*   *   *   *   *   *   *

When the boys awoke the next morning the sun was streaming down on their sleeping place with a strength that showed that it had been up some time. With a start Frank sat up and looked about him.

What was the matter with him? His eyes felt heavy and his throat was parched. In his ears, too, there was a wild ringing sound and his limbs felt stiff and inert. Shouting to the others, who were gazing about them in a bewildered sort of way, Frank described his symptoms.

They all felt as badly as he did.

"I feel like I'd been boiled in the ship's boiler along with the cook's dish-rags," announced Ben Stubbs.

Even old Sikaso shook his head mournfully and said that he didn't feel at all well.

"I wonder how old man Barr feels?" said the irreverent Billy rubbing his red-rimmed eyes.

The next minute there was a shout of astonishment from them all.

Mr. Barr's blankets were empty and he was nowhere to be seen about the camp!

Forgetting their painful feelings in the shock of this discovery the boys hastened to the river bank to see if by any chance he was down at the steam launch.

The launch, too, was missing!

With a cry of rage Ben Stubbs shook his fist down the river.

"I see it all, boys," he exclaimed. "The old scallywag drugged us - doped us - that's why we feel so badly and - "

"Howling bob-cats! I'll bet he's stolen a march on us and got away with the ivory," - this was Billy.

There was a rush for the spot in which the precious stuff had been cached.

A few broken tusks lay there.

But of the great hoard that the Boy Aviators had worked so faithfully to salvage not a vestige remained.

"Bilked, by the great hornspoon!" yelled Ben.

"But not beaten yet," was Frank's calm rejoinder. "Come on, boys, we've got to be stirring. Barr's got a long start of us, but we'll get him yet. Ben, you and Sikaso will take one of the Arabs' canoes - the ones they left at the river bank when they started after us - Harry, Billy, Lathrop and I will fly to the coast in the Golden Eagle II. We've just enough gasoline."

"All right, sir," said Ben, touching his forelock with an old sailor trick - a token of respect involuntarily forced from him by Frank's manly promptitude in taking the bull by the horns, "We're with you to the last ditch, the top of the main-top gallant, the bottom of the deep-blue sea, or the ends of the earth."

"That goes for us too, Frank," supplemented Billy.

"And count me in on that," cried Lathrop.

As for Harry, he gripped his brother's hand and the boys at once set about their preparations to outwit their treacherous enemy. In the midst of their bustle an interruption as utterly unexpected as it was for a moment alarming occurred.

The bushes parted and from them there stepped no less a person than Muley-Hassan.

He was followed a minute later by half-a-dozen fatigued-looking followers.

The boys' hands flew to their revolvers and Ben grabbed up a rifle. Sikaso's ever-ready axe was in the air in a second.

But the Arab put up his hand.

"I have not come to fight but to bargain," he said.

"You have beaten me at every point of the game. Diego is dead - "

"Dead," cried Frank.

"He was bitten by an adder as we were vainly searching for the ivory," said the Arab sadly, "he died almost instantly."

Of course the boys felt no sorrow for the death of the treacherous scamp and did not pretend to. They had no great reason to love Muley-Hassan either, so Frank said coldly:

"What is it you want?"

"Permission to take my canoes and leave this cursed country forever."

Frank waved toward the river.

"Your canoes are where you left them the night you made the cowardly attack on our camp. You can have them all but one. That one we need."

"Alas," sighed the Arab, "I do not need as many as I did when I came. Of all my followers these alone remain."

He pointed to the scant six, skinny, fever-stricken wretches who stood behind him.

"Good-by," said the stately Arab, holding out his hand in farewell, "we shall never meet again, but I shall ever remember that you dealt by me far better than I would have dealt by you."

"At all events you have one good deed to look back to in your life," exclaimed the impulsive Billy.

The Arab looked at him questioningly.

"You saved George Desmond's life," said the reporter shortly.

"That was many years ago," said the Arab with a start of recognition at the name of the dead explorer, "I have changed since."

With a wave of the hand he strode to the river's edge and half-an-hour later he and the remnant of his band were out of sight round a bend in the upper river.

At almost the same instant the boys soared aloft in the Golden Eagle II, and the chase for the ivory was on.

Below the flying aeroplane Ben Stubbs and old Sikaso - the latter as silent as ever - paddled down the river in silence.

It was a time for deeds, not talk.

CHAPTER XXIII

ABOARD "THE BRIGAND"

The Brigand, a black, schooner-rigged yacht of about 1800 tons, with a yellow funnel amidships, and flying the red and blue burgee of the Transatlantic Yacht Club, lay at anchor on the rolling blue swells off the harbor of Assini in the early dawn of the day following the treachery of Luther Barr. Her crew - for the most part a riff-raff collection picked up in a hurry, for the old man had only made up his mind to make his daring grab for the ivory at the last minute - lolled about the decks idly. There was no one aboard to give command, for Jack Halsey, the mate who had been in command since the death of the captain had gone ashore the night before.

As old Barr had prophesied, the mate's love for strong liquor had overcome him and he was now lying hopelessly intoxicated in a low drinking den. The raw "trade gin" that he had drunk had rendered him insensible and so he would remain for many hours to come.

Some sort of animation diffused itself among the crew as they saw a low-laden launch headed toward them from the shore. In it were seated Luther Barr and several negroes including the black captain.

"Here, you lazy loafers!" hailed Barr, who was evidently in a bad temper and also in a furious hurry, as the launch ranged alongside, "bear a hand here and rig a sling and get this stuff aboard."

The "stuff" referred to was the priceless collection of ivory which lay higgeldy-piggeldy in the bottom of the launch just as it had been thrown in by the negroes in Barr's pay. Anticipating that the boys would put up a stiff fight for the ivory he had taken the precaution to hire these ne'er-do-wells, who would do anything, from cutting a throat to stealing a chicken, for pay. Barr had paid them well and when he had arrived at the camp he had taken the precaution to leave them down the river about half-a-mile while he went on alone with the launch and her captain to see how the land lay. When he realized that the boys were not fooled by his forged order from Mr. Beasley he decided to use the chloroform he had bought for just such an emergency, and then rousing his followers when the boys were drugged it had not taken long with their united efforts to load the ivory.

Urged on by Barr's promise of a large reward the captain of the launch had spun his little vessel down the river at top speed and thus had been able to make the coast in record time.

"Where in thunder is that mate Halsey?" roared Barr as he saw the bos'n - a seedy-looking fellow from the London slums - taking charge of the transfer of the ivory from the launch to the deck of the Brigand.

"He went ashore last night," rejoined the other.

"And I suppose he is helplessly drunk now," raged

Barr. "How in the name of fortune are we going to get the yacht out of here?"

"Wait till he gets sober," was the bos'n's grunted reply as the men hastily transferred the last of the precious freight of tusks to the Brigand's deck.

Barr jumped to the accommodation ladder and was aboard in a second, despite his apparent feebleness. His face was distorted with rage and cupidity.

"We have got to get out of here at once - now do you understand?" he roared, crazed with rage.

"I'll give a thousand dollars to the man that will get me out of this harbor and well off to sea."

"If it comes to that I guess I can take a chance of navigating the yacht even if I don't hold a master's ticket," replied the bos'n.

"But are you a navigator?" questioned Barr eagerly

"Well, Mr. Barr, I held a master's ticket once before drink got me and I piled my ship on a reef," was the answer.

"You're good enough for me!" shouted Barr overjoyed, "and now we'll up anchor and get away from this abominable coast."

He scanned the sky shoreward anxiously. He did not confide to his new captain, however, the fact that at any moment he expected to see swift vengeance in the shape of the Golden Eagle II pursuing him.

With the roustabout crew that had been shipped in New York from a West Street boarding-master it took some time to get the anchor broken out - the men going at their work sulkily. At last, however, it was "up and down" as the sailors say, and Luther Barr himself signaled on the engine-room telegraph "Full speed, ahead." The engines of the yacht begin to revolve and the crafty old pillager almost gave a cry of joy as he felt the vibration beneath his feet.

The Boy Aviators could not cross the Atlantic in the aeroplane and there would not be a ship leaving the coast for a month.

Luther Barr chuckled.

He had beaten the boys at their own game.

By the time they arrived in New York the ivory would have been sold in London and he would be traveling in Europe on his ill-earned gains. That Beasley (his unsuspecting partner) would be ruined gave the money-crazed old man no care at all.

But even as the launch cast loose from the moving yacht and headed back to the shore - her occupants greedily fingering the bills Barr had given them for their work - Barr, from his station on the bridge, gave a start and an exclamation.

High in the air, and not more than ten miles inland, a black object that looked like a huge bird, but which Barr knew in his guilty soul was the Golden Eagle II, was rapidly winging its way toward them.

"More steam," he shouted down the tube to the

engineer and the yacht, a long creamy wave curving away from her sharp black bow, began to move even faster.

"What are we making?" Barr asked eagerly of the late bos'n who, binoculars in hand, was taking the ship out through the treacherous harbor entrance as confidently as if he were once more a captain.

"Twelve knots," was the reply.

"We must do better," raged Barr.

"Impossible!" was the answer. "We are risking the yacht now. I am not familiar with this harbor and there are shoals and reefs all about us stretching many miles out to sea. At any moment, unless we proceed cautiously, we may run aground. Five knots would suit me better than twelve."

Barr chafed silently. The reply was unanswerable.

Better to go slow than to run the ship ashore. Suddenly he snatched the binoculars from the man beside him and turned them on the aeroplane. He almost uttered a cry of triumph as the craft swung into his field of vision.

There was something the matter with her.

She was no longer rushing straight ahead.

As Luther Barr watched her he saw the great aircraft swoop in a huge circle above the town and then settle down so swiftly that it looked as if she must have been dashed to pieces. But the town was hidden behind a point and he could not see it.

"I hope she has been dashed to pieces," he gritted between his teeth savagely, "that would mean the saving of a lot of trouble for me."

But even as he prepared to put the binoculars back in the pocket alongside the binnacle with an evil smile playing about his thin lips, there came a startling shock.

Barr was almost thrown from his feet and only saved himself from falling by grasping a stanchion. The ship quivered from stem to stern as if she had been hit a staggering blow.

"We've struck a reef!" exclaimed the late bos'n.

"A reef!" yelled Barr, beside himself with fury.

"I told you we would if you insisted on keeping up such a speed," angrily replied the other.

Beside himself with rage Barr picked up a heavy belaying pin to which, the signal halyards had been attached and struck the man before him a terrible blow with it.

Fortunately for his intended victim - for Barr in his rage would not have cared had he killed him - he ducked just in time and the blow was a glancing one. The man came at him like a tiger, but Barr, quick as a flash, slid his hand into his coat pocket.

"If you advance a step nearer I'll blow your brains out," he said coldly.

There was a glitter in his eyes that showed he meant what he said and with a muttered:

"I'll get even with you, Barr, as sure as my name is Al Davis," the late captain of the Brigand left the bridge.

Barr's active mind was at work at once planning schemes to get the ivory off immediately. Accustomed to crises of all kinds, the recent scene with the man Davis hadn't even warmed his chilly blood.

Calling the engineer he ordered an immediate inspection to be made. The result was discouraging. The Brigand lay with her bow hard and fast on a low sunken reef and while there was no apparent leak the chief engineer shook his head at the vessel's plight.

That there was grave danger was evidenced a short while after when the fire-room force - which had been ordered to keep steam up in the hope of backing the ship off later - came pouring on deck crying that there was three feet of water in the fire-room.

"That settles it," said the chief. "We are on a doomed ship."

"The boats! The boats!" shouted the men.

"Stay where you are," bellowed Barr, mad with rage, "get that ivory off first."

"To blazes with your ivory," shouted a grizzled old fireman, "do you think we are going to perish aboard here for such an old skinflint as you?"

"Why, if we had time we'd run you up at your own

main-gaff you old land-shark," shouted another.

"Come on! the boats - the boats!" they yelled.

Barr stood irresolute while they lowered the four boats that the Brigand carried and piled into them. The shore was only a few miles off and they would reach it in a few hours.

While Barr hesitated he felt the ship give a lurch. She was settling!

That decided him.

Ivory or no ivory he feared such a death as he felt convinced would come to any one unfortunate enough to be aboard the ship in a few hours' time even more than he did the loss of the ivory.

"Hold on!" he shouted to the men in the boats, "I'm coming along."

"Not much you ain't," yelled Davis - the man he had dealt the blow to, "you stay there and rot with your ivory - you old crook."

With mocking laughs the men pulled away and Luther Barr, master of millions, was left alone on the sinking yacht.

CHAPTER XXIV

THE BOY AVIATORS HOLD A WINNING HAND

The cause of the sudden swoop of the Golden Eagle II that Barr had seen from the yacht with such satisfaction was the need of replenishing her gasoline tank. The big craft landed in the dusty public square of the city where pretty well every one in the town was on hand when her runners and pneumatic tired supporting wheels struck the ground. The young adventurers were out of her in a few minutes and the first man to grasp their hands was M. Desplaines.

"I am delighted to see you," he exclaimed, "but if you anticipated catching Luther Barr you are too late."

"We saw his yacht steaming out to sea," rejoined Frank, "but if only we can get more gasoline we can catch him yet."

"What, you mean to pursue him?"

"We certainly do. He has stolen the ivory that we recovered at so much risk to ourselves."

"I didn't realize, of course, what your errand was," said M. Desplaines in reply, "till Mr. Barr arrived here in his yacht the other day and informed me that you had stolen a cache of ivory belonging to him and asked my aid to help in capturing you. I had no means of disproving his story so I lent him the steam launch, but I see now by his action in hastening to the yacht that he is, as you say, the real thief."

Hastily Frank told a part of their adventures and if he had had any remaining doubt of the boys' sincerity the consular agent was soon convinced of the truth of their story and of the villainy of Barr.

"I can get you some gasoline - ," he said. "A merchant here in town recently bought a launch and as the freight boats do not touch in here often he has laid in a large supply of the fuel. I have no doubt that at my request he will be glad to sell you as much as you require."

This was good news indeed, and the boys hastened round to the house of M. Desplaine's friend. To their unspeakable regret, however, he was absent on a fishing expedition in his launch.

"If that isn't tough luck," exclaimed Billy disgustedly, "what can we do now?"

"Wait till he gets back or else break into his warehouse," said Harry.

"We cannot commit burglary," said Frank, "we shall have to wait."

M. Desplaines invited the party to lunch at his house but as may be imagined they did not eat much. Each was in too much of a hurry to ascertain if the fisherman had not returned. Immediately the meal was dispatched, therefore, they hastened out into the street andhere they encountered a strange scene.

A score or more of rough-looking characters had just landed from four ship's boats that lay moored at the small wharf. They had joined forces with the crew of the launch that had aided in the ivory hunt and all were bent on a carouse. The boys were hardly able to speak from excitement when they read on the stern of each of the boats the words "Brigand N. Y."

"Those boats are from Barr's yacht," cried Frank.

"So they are," cried M. Desplaines, "and from some of these men perhaps we shall be able to hear what has happened."

It was an easy matter to get the story from the crew.

The only trouble was they all wanted to talk at once. Bit by bit, however, the boys got the story and learned that the Brigand was sinking with a big hole in her bottom. While the others were talking a tall man, who formed part of the crew that had just landed, beckoned Frank aside:

"Come here, young master," he said, "I want a word with you. You are one of the Boy Aviators?"

"I am!" replied Frank, "who are you?"

"My name's Al Davis; I was a skipper once - but never mind that now. But if you want to make a piece of money out of salvage I'll tell you how if you make it worth my while."

"What is it you have to tell me?" asked Frank.

For reply the man put his hand up to Frank's ear and whispered cautiously.

"Is that worth anything?" he asked after he had imparted the information.

"Well I should say so," cried Frank joyously, and he slipped the man a bill of large denomination.

"I'll buy everybody a drink," shouted Davis, shuffling off.

"Come on, boys, we've no time to lose!" Frank exclaimed the next minute and they hastened round to the house of M. Desplaines' friend.

This time that worthy was at home and greeted them warmly. He had a plentiful stock of gasoline more than enough, he said - and he gladly sold them all they wanted.

In a few minutes the Golden Eagle II's main and reserve tanks were replenished to the full and the boys were ready for a record flight to the wreck.

So far Frank had not divulged to the others what his information concerning the wreck was that he had received from Davis, and he did not now though he felt sorely tempted to.

Amid cheers from the crowd the Golden Eagle II, with all the adventurers aboard, soared once more into the air; but this time headed out to sea. They had not risen a hundred feet before they sighted the wreck, which had struck round a low point out of sight from the town. She lay, a dismal-looking object, heeled over to one side; but Frank saw, to his intense joy, that there was still a feeble curl of smoke coming from her stack.

This meant that the water had not yet extinguished her fires and was favorable to the daring plan he had conceived.

As the Golden Eagle II drew nearer, the figure of old Luther Barr could be plainly seen rushing about on the upper bridge.

He seemed demented with terror.

"Save me! save me! the ship is going down!" he cried in agonized tones, as a few minutes later the aeroplane swung in big circles above his head.

The boys, despite their righteous anger at the wicked old man, yet could not help feeling some pity mingled with their amusement as the old coward ran about the bridge like a crazy man.

"We'll get you off if you'll agree to do something for us," hailed Frank through his megaphone as the aeroplane soared in big circles round the wreck and the distracted old man.

"Anything, anything!" cried back old Barr piteously.

"Will you sign a release for the ivory you stole from us, admitting your theft?" asked Frank.

"Yes, yes, my boys. I'll sign anything, but get me off. I don't want to die like this. Oh this is a terrible end!"

"What are you going to do, Frank?" asked Billy, as the Golden Eagle II, in obedience to Frank's controlling hand, began to drop.

"You see that sand bank that the falling tide has exposed," was Frank's reply.

They all nodded.

"I am going to land there and we can wade through the water to the yacht. I judge the water isn't more than three feet deep at the deepest part."

The landing was made without a hitch - the sand being of the hard-ribbed variety that covers the numerous reefs along the west African coast.

After a short interval of wading the boys stood on the deck of the Brigand, where she hung on the edge of the reef. Frank's sharp eyes noticed that except for her forefoot the vessel was in deep water, as the reef dropped off quite abruptly.

Old Barr received them with almost hysterical joy.

"This is better than I deserve, boys; better than I deserve," he kept repeating.

"You had better stop your sniveling," said Frank sharply, thoroughly disgusted with the cowardly old rascal. "Where are pens, ink and paper?"

The ivory merchant led the way to the chart-house. "Be quick, boys - she might sink," he stuttered.

The document that Frank dictated, Luther Barr signed

and the others witnessed, read like this:

I, Luther Barr, of New York, do here by deed, make over and assign to the Boy Aviators - namely Frank and Harry Chester, William Barnes and Lathrop Beasley, all my share, claim or equity in the ivory which I wrongfully stole from them, which fact I with shame acknowledge. I hereby affix my signature which I admit in the presence of witnesses to be my true manner of signing."

"Now," said Frank, "just to show we are not mean, there is some ivory left in the Moon Mountains, near the spot which is indicated on your map. Sikaso, a faithful Krooman, hid it for us when we could not carry it away. If you find it you can have it."

The old man rubbed his hands in greedy glee.

"Oh thank you, boys; thank you, I'll find it, I'll find it," he croaked, his wrinkled old face wreathed in smiles.

"Lathrop," ordered Frank, "you and Billy take Mr. Barr back to shore. Harry and I will stay here.

"We have a lot to do. Leave the Golden Eagle ashore to be packed and forwarded later. Hurry back in the launch."

"What are you going to do?" demanded Barr.

"I think that your interest in our movements ceased with the signing of this paper," rejoined Frank.

At that moment the Brigand gave a violent shudder as if she was indeed about to go down. With a shrill scream of terror old Barr ran out on deck and hastily clambered down on to the reef. From there he waded with Billy and Lathrop to the Golden Eagle II, and was taken ashore.

"Now then to work," said Frank as the aeroplane winged her way shoreward with their enemy.

"What are you going to do?" demanded Harry in an astonished tone. There didn't seem to be much to do to his mind but wait till they were taken off the stranded yacht by the launch.

"You'll see," replied Frank. "In the first place, Harry, the Brigand was never in any danger of sinking. She is as sound as a dollar."

"Are you crazy?" cried Harry, "why there's a lot of water in her engine-room. She must have sprung a leak as big as a house."

Frank laughed.

"There are more ways of killing a cat than by choking it with cream," was his cryptic remark. "What would you say if I told you that in an hour's time we, will have every drop of water out of the yacht, and that following that we will have her afloat again at high-water."

"That you are a marvel."

"Well, it's going to happen - come with me."

Frank led the way to the engine-room.

"Luckily I know something about marine engines since we took that trip on the gun boat in Nicaragua."

He examined the gauges. They showed sixty pounds of steam still in the boilers.

"Not much - but enough," was Frank's comment. He then turned to two valve wheels on the working platform and started to screw them up.

"What in the world are you doing?" asked Harry.

"Closing the sea-cocks which were opened by Al Davis, the former bos'n, in revenge for a blow Luther Barr struck him when the ship went aground," was Frank's astonishing reply.

"But how in thunder do you know about that?"

"Davis told me while you were trying to get something out of those fellows who were all gabbling at once."

"And when you have closed up the sea-cocks?"

"Then I shall start the centrifugal pumps going to empty the engine-room, and we'll soon have her as sound as a dollar."

Luckily the water had not, as Frank had surmised, reached the fires, and though low there was enough pressure of steam t o run the pumps till the boys were able to work in the stoke-hold. Then both boys set to work with a will and soon had the furnaces going full-blast, and the steam gauges registered seventy, then eighty and then one hundred and fifty pounds.

"There, that will do," exclaimed Frank, as, pretty well tuckered out, they threw aside their shovels. "Now we have to wait for the tide and reinforcements."

They had not long to wait.

Of course at the height the tide now was the reef was pretty well covered and it would have been impossible to make a landing in the air-ship, so Billy had chartered the power launch of the friend who had sold them the gasoline.

Ben Stubbs and Sikaso, who had arrived late that' afternoon, were on board the little craft and Ben's loud "Ahoy!" brought the Boy Aviators to the rail on the jump - waving and shouting greetings.

But there were others in the launch, and among them the boys spied several faces of bronzed men who looked thorough seamen. M. Desplaines, who was in the launch, explained that they had formed part of the crew of a steamer that had been wrecked down the coast some weeks previously. They had been waiting for a ship and were willing to work their passage home: to New York. Among them was their captain, a good seaman and a former yacht skipper.

"But - but," said Frank amazedly, as the men piled on board and the boys all shook hands madly with everybody. "We can't take this yacht - it isn't ours, we have no right."

M. Desplaines held out a piece of paper; smiling as he did so. It was covered with writing in Luther Barr's cramped hand and was a characteristic document. Stripped of its legal phraseology it was an agreement to the effect that if the boys would make no salvage charges for saving the yacht, they could have her free of cost to sail back to New York.

"But," said Frank, "how did he know we intended to save her?"

"'The man Davis got boisterously drunk and when arrested admitted that the yacht was in no danger and that he had flooded her stoke-hold out of revenge," explained M. Desplaines.

"In that case, why does not Mr. Barr come back to New York on her?" demanded Frank.

The consular agent smiled.

"He thinks he is on the track of more ivory and has already engaged part of an expedition," he replied. "To tell you the truth, his anxiety to save expense on the yacht has had quite as much to do with his loaning her to you as anything else. He expects you to pay the crew. If you wish to go back to New York on this yacht I will have your aeroplane dismantled and forwarded by freight."

"Well," laughed Frank, "will we, boys?"

"I should say we will!" came in a chorus.

"And steam back to old New York?"

"You bet."

As Frank had anticipated, at flood-tide the yacht was backed off under her own power and then came the time for farewells - and warm ones they were. To Sikaso the boys presented a rifle and an automatic revolver as the noble old fellow would not hear of taking money. The last glimpse they had of their black friend, as the yacht headed due west for America, he was standing gloomily in the stern of the launch - one hand on his faithful axe and the other raised against the blue sky as if in benediction.

"Well," said Frank, as the distance shut out the picture, "we are bound for home at last."

"What ever will they say when they hear of our adventures?" cried Harry.

"And the recovery of the ivory?" chimed in Lathrop, "my father's business is saved. We must cable from the Canaries of our success."

"And the narrative of George Desmond and our own experiences with the Flying Men?" chimed in Billy.

"Oh, you'll have to can that rarebit dream!" cried Harry.

"I will not!" exclaimed Billy indignantly. "I'm going to print it."

"On the funny page maybe. I'd like to see the newspaper that would publish such a yarn."

sAlas for poor Billy! Harry was right.

Nobody would believe his strange tale and last he grew tired of telling it, and even to hardly credit it himself.

As for George Desmond's time-yellowed pages they repose in the Smithsonian Institute, and after a learned wrangle between savants of all countries - lasting many months - it was agreed that the poor explorer must have lost his mind and that the narrative of the Flying Men was the offspring of a brain crazed by suffering.

"It's a strange termination to our adventures to be steaming home on Barr's yacht," said Frank, after a long pause in which they had all gazed back at the fast dimming shore of the Dark Continent.

"I should say so," cried Lathrop. "It's as near as I ever want to
get to him, too."

"Same here," joined in Billy, "but I don't suppose we shall ever hear from him again."

But Billy was wrong.

The boys did hear from Luther Barr again and in an extraordinary manner. The malevolent old man was to be the cause of some surprising adventures in which the boys at the risk of their lives were once more pitted against powerful enemies.

With what flying colors they emerged from their dangers, difficulties and adventures will be told in the next volume of this series - "THE BOY AVIATORS' TREASURE QUEST; or THE GOLDEN GALLEON."

Choose from Thousands of 1stWorldLibrary Classics By

Adolphus WilliamWard
Aesop
Agatha Christie
Alexander Aaronsohn
Alexander Kielland
Alexandre Dumas
Alfred Gatty
Alfred Ollivant
Alice Duer Miller
Alice Turner Curtis
Alice Dunbar
Ambrose Bierce
Amelia E. Barr
Andrew Lang
Andrew McFarland Davis
Anna Sewell
Annie Besant
Annie Hamilton Donnell
Annie Payson Call
Anton Chekhov
Arnold Bennett
Arthur Conan Doyle
Arthur Ransome
Atticus
B. M. Bower
Basil King
Bayard Taylor
Ben Macomber
Booth Tarkington
Bram Stoker
C. Collodi
C. E. Orr
C. M. Ingleby
Carolyn Wells
Catherine Parr Traill
Charles A. Eastman
Charles Dickens
Charles Dudley Warner
Charles Farrar Browne
Charles Ives
Charles Kingsley
Charles Lathrop Pack
Charles Whibley
Charles Willing Beale
Charlotte M. Braeme
Charlotte M.Yonge
Clair W. Hayes
Clarence Day Jr.
Clarence E. Mulford

Clemence Housman
Confucius
Cornelis DeWitt Wilcox
Cyril Burleigh
D. H. Lawrence
Daniel Defoe
David Garnett
Don Carlos Janes
Donald Keyhole
Dorothy Kilner
Dougan Clark
E. Nesbit
E.P.Roe
E. Phillips Oppenheim
Edgar Allan Poe
Edgar Rice Burroughs
Edith Wharton
Edward J. O'Biren
John Cournos
Edwin L. Arnold
Eleanor Atkins
Elizabeth Cleghorn
Gaskell
Elizabeth Von Arnim
Ellem Key
Emily Dickinson
Erasmus W. Jones
Ernie Howard Pie
Ethel Turner
Ethel Watts Mumford
Eugenie Foa
Eugene Wood
Evelyn Everett-Green
Everard Cotes
F. J. Cross
Federick Austin Ogg
Ferdinand Ossendowski
Francis Bacon
Francis Darwin
Frances Hodgson Burnett
Frank Gee Patchin
Frank Harris
Frank Jewett Mather
Frank L. Packard
Frederick Trevor Hill
Frederick Winslow Taylor
Friedrich Kerst
Friedrich Nietzsche
Fyodor Dostoyevsky

Gabrielle E. Jackson
Garrett P. Serviss
Gaston Leroux
George Ade
Geroge Bernard Shaw
George Ebers
George Eliot
George MacDonald
George Orwell
George Tucker
George W. Cable
George Wharton James
Gertrude Atherton
Grace E. King
Grant Allen
Guillermo A. Sherwell
Gulielma Zollinger
Gustav Flaubert
H. A. Cody
H. B. Irving
H. G. Wells
H. H. Munro
H. Irving Hancock
H. Rider Haggard
H. W. C. Davis
Hamilton Wright Mabie
Hans Christian Andersen
Harold Avery
Harold McGrath
Harriet Beecher Stowe
Harry Houidini
Helent Hunt Jackson
Helen Nicolay
Hendy David Thoreau
Henrik Ibsen
Henry Adams
Henry Ford
Henry Frost
Henry James
Henry Jones Ford
Henry Seton Merriman
Henry Wadsworth
Longfellow
Henry W Longfellow
Herbert A. Giles
Herbert N. Casson
Herman Hesse
Homer
Honore De Balzac

Horace Walpole
Horatio Alger, Jr.
Howard Pyle
Howard R. Garis
Hugh Lofting
Hugh Walpole
Humphry Ward
Ian Maclaren
Israel Abrahams
J.G.Austin
J. Henri Fabre
J. M. Barrie
J. Macdonald Oxley
J. S. Knowles
J. Storer Clouston
Jack London
Jacob Abbott
James Allen
James Lane Allen
James Andrews
James Baldwin
James DeMille
James Joyce
James Oliver Curwood
James Oppenheim
James Otis
Jane Austen
Jens Peter Jacobsen
Jerome K. Jerome
John Burroughs
John F. Kennedy
John Gay
John Glasworthy
John Habberton
John Joy Bell
John Milton
John Philip Sousa
Jonathan Swift
Joseph Carey
Joseph Conrad
Joseph Jacobs
Julian Hawthrone
Julies Vernes
Justin Huntly McCarthy
Kakuzo Okakura
Kenneth Grahame
Kate Langley Bosher
L. A. Abbot
L. T. Meade
L. Frank Baum
Laura Lee Hope

Laurence Housman
Leo Tolstoy
Leonid Andreyev
Lewis Carroll
Lilian Bell
Lloyd Osbourne
Louis Tracy
Louisa May Alcott
Lucy Fitch Perkins
Lucy Maud Montgomery
Lydia Miller Middleton
Lyndon Orr
M. H. Adams
Margaret E. Sangster
Margaret Vandercook
Maria Edgeworth
Maria Thompson Daviess
Mariano Azuela
Marion Polk Angellotti
Mark Overton
Mark Twain
Mary Austin
Mary Cole
Mary Rowlandson
Mary Wollstonecraft Shelley
Max Beerbohm
Myra Kelly
Nathaniel Hawthrone
O. F. Walton
Oscar Wilde
Owen Johnson
P.G.Wodehouse
Paul and Mable Thorn
Paul G. Tomlinson
Paul Severing
Peter B. Kyne
Plato
R. Derby Holmes
R. L. Stevenson
Rabindranath Tagore
Rahul Alvares
Ralph Waldo Emmerson
Rene Descartes
Rex E. Beach
Richard Harding Davis
Richard Jefferies
Robert Barr
Robert Frost
Robert Gordon Anderson
Robert L. Drake

Robert Lansing
Robert Michael Ballantyne
Robert W. Chambers
Rosa Nouchette Carey
Ross Kay
Rudyard Kipling
Samuel B. Allison
Samuel Hopkins Adams
Sarah Bernhardt
Selma Lagerlof
Sherwood Anderson
Sigmund Freud
Standish O'Grady
Stanley Weyman
Stella Benson
Stephen Crane
Stewart Edward White
Stijn Streuvels
Swami Abhedananda
Swami Parmananda
T. S. Ackland
The Princess Der Ling
Thomas A. Janvier
Thomas A Kempis
Thomas Anderton
Thomas Bailey Aldrich
Thomas Bulfinch
Thomas De Quincey
Thomas H. Huxley
Thomas Hardy
Thomas More
Thornton W. Burgess
U. S. Grant
Valentine Williams
Victor Appleton
Virginia Woolf
Walter Scott
Washington Irving
Wilbur Lawton
Wilkie Collins
Willa Cather
Willard F. Baker
William Makepeace Thackeray
William W. Walter
Winston Churchill
Yei Theodora Ozaki
Young E. Allison
Zane Grey

www.ingramcontent.com/pod-product-compliance
Lightning Source LLC
Chambersburg PA
CBHW050035180626
46810CB00002B/729